MONTANA ROSE

DEANN SMALLWOOD

SOUL MATE PUBLISHING

New York

MONTANA ROSE

Copyright©2016

DEANN SMALLWOOD

Cover Design by Victoria Vane

Published in the United States of America by

Soul Mate Publishing

P.O. Box 24

Macedon, New York, 14502

ISBN: 978-1-68291-254-6

ebook ISBN: 978-1-68291-060-3

www.SoulMatePublishing.com

Books by DeAnn Smallwood

Unconquerable Callie
Tears in the Wind
Wyoming Heather
One Shingle to Hang
Montana Man
Montana Rose

Writing as D.M. Woods:

Death Crosses the Finish Line
Death Is a Habit

To the memory of my beloved grandmother,

Tina Mae Duplice.

She met each challenge life threw at her

with spirit and inner beauty.

I was blessed to have her in my life.

She was the blueprint for Rose.

And as always to my husband, Marvin.

He's there through my long hours

when I live in my mind,

and my writer's ups and downs.

He's the wind beneath my wings.

And to the memory of my darling Jesse.

You will live forever in my heart.

Acknowledgements

Thank you, Debby, and Soul Mate Publishing for your continued faith in me. Debby, my work, my books are always safe in your capable and caring hands. You make me believe in myself.

Thanks to Lynda Coleman, queen of editors. I covet your magic pen and ability to seek out all my errors and poor punctuation. You're a real find.

And thanks to all my friends at St. Ann's. Your faith in me is amazing.

Chapter 1

1860 Wise River, Montana

Rose tucked the bank draft into her drawstring purse as she boarded the train. It wasn't enough. But then, would any amount of money be enough to compensate for her failure? Her wide skirt brushed the sides of the seats, the hem collecting dust from the narrow, gritty aisle. It was beyond her to care.

Heaviness had entered her body the moment she signed the deed to the small homestead, selling it to the owner of the ranch bordering her few acres. King Ranch. Well, the name suited. The king did indeed rule, sweeping the Wyoming country with a heavy-handed scepter, a monarch with the money and patience to wait her out. Then, like a spider, it pounced and sucked her land into its web of acreage never to emerge.

She adjusted the hat with the ridiculous robin perched on a nest of russet-colored leaves. It sat atop her blonde curls, a foolish attempt to thumb her nose at defeat. She may be beaten, but she was still fashionable.

Rose sniffed, taking small comfort from the defiant act and took the seat by the window. She rubbed the smudged window as the train pulled out of the station then closed her eyes, blocking out the dusty town and her dreams.

One year. She had made it one year. Her sister Wisteria's words replayed in her mind. *"If anyone can make a go of homesteading, it will be you, Rose. But you are a woman alone."*

Rose felt heat rise to her cheeks as she recalled how she'd scoffed at Wisteria's worries.

If the devil kept score, surely she'd get points for trying. Trying and not complaining. Living in the small soddy where even the slightest task was backbreaking. And she'd loved it. That was the worst part, she'd loved it. Loved the independence, the small accomplishments, the reward of a beautiful sunrise after a storm, and the solitude.

A slight smile crept across her face. Her memories took her back so totally she could smell the sage and see the sun glinting off the backs of the cattle. She could feel the ever-present breeze ruffling her hair, and the sun coaxing out more freckles, dusting her pert nose.

Her throat tightened. She also could just as easily remember the bodies, bloating in the summer heat. Her herd, her entire herd, wiped out by tick fever. The scourge had rampaged throughout the valley, indiscriminately hitting both small and large ranches. The smaller ones, like hers, had gone under, unable to replace cattle and start again. The larger spreads absorbed the loss and plodded on. Ranches like the King Ranch profited, gobbling up the surrounding properties. What did it matter old-timers marveled they'd never seen the like? Marveling didn't pay the bills or restock the ranch.

Rose gave a deep sigh. In fairness, she'd received a fair price for the land. But nothing could pay for the lost year. And it was for darned sure nothing could pay for the cold lump of utter defeat lodged beneath her breasts.

Both of her sisters, Wisteria and Petunia, had offered her their homes as refuge. Both were newly married, and although they assured her she would not be intruding, Rose knew she would be. Petunia, the oldest of the three, had married a wealthy banker late in life. They lived in Chicago, which offered her city life in all its splendor. She would die inch by inch, day by day, breathing the stale air and having no other purpose in life other than deciding what dress to wear for what occasion.

Rose opened her eyes and tugged off her once-white gloves, exposing callused hands and broken nails. Grimacing, she quickly sought back the gloves' concealment. She was right to refuse Petunia's kindness. She'd be like a thistle among roses.

She also knew Wisteria had understood her reluctance to join her and Ben in Montana. They were happily established in Wise River. Ben loved every moment of being reunited with his family, and he was practicing medicine. They had wasted no time in adopting Robin, Rose's niece. Now, all the couple had to do was get her to call Ben 'Daddy' instead of the lisping, 'En. Theirs was a happy nest with no room for a dispirited woman, one who lacked the will to move forward.

Losing her much-older husband had been a test, but it no way compared to this loss. Rose felt as though she were a husk of her former, determined self.

Still, when Wisteria's letter arrived, Rose had quickly grasped the lifeline. *Rose, marvelous news. Our schoolteacher has decided to move. There's an opening, and not only that, there's an attached living quarters to the school. You'll be able to maintain the independence that's so important to you. Ben assures me that the position is yours if you want it. He talked to the school board and has been given permission to offer you the job. I'm not sure of the pay, probably not much. But it's a start. Take it, Rose, and use it as a place to heal. I know it's selfish, but to have you here in Wise River would be frosting on my cake. Actually, it would be seven-minute icing. Remember you and I fighting over the bowl and demanding Petunia not scrape it so clean?*

Rose telegraphed Wisteria her 'yes' and here she was sitting on a train headed for Wise River, Montana. Even though she knew nothing about being a teacher.

Chapter 2

The train chugged off, leaving Rose standing on the wooden platform, surrounded by a puddle of bags. She glanced around. Where was Ben? Wisteria? Hadn't they gotten her telegraph? She hadn't been thinking clearly when she'd sent it. Actually, she hadn't been thinking clearly since selling the homestead, but she was sure she'd told them she was arriving today, Tuesday. Then she chided herself for giving in to the panic filling her. They had been detained. That was all. Simply detained. Ben probably had an emergency and they'd be here shortly. Rose fought back at her rising panic.

Resolutely, she picked up one of the smaller bags and turned toward the station house. One last time, she searched the area. No, no one waiting for her. The only other people were a man and a boy, loading a rather cumbersome trunk onto a wagon. They were at the other end of the platform, but Rose couldn't help but notice that they weren't working in harmony.

The boy appeared sullen and kicked at the trunk before trying to pick up his end. The man barked something at him, then shoved the boy aside and loaded the entire trunk by himself. Rose gave an intake of breath as the man's shirt tightened across his back and muscles rippled. Her eyes were riveted as the man tipped back his black, wide-brimmed hat, and wiped his sleeve across his face. Thick, brown hair, the rich brownness of a mink's pelt, fell across his forehead then curled on his neck, a haircut long overdue.

Before she could move, the boy stalked past, throwing her a cursory glance. His sneer was emphasized by the coldness in his eyes. He was a big boy, and no doubt would someday equal the size of the man Rose assumed was his father. She guessed him to be ten or eleven years of age.

Shrugging off his belligerent demeanor, Rose opened the station house door. They were none of her concern. She had all she could handle with her own life. Hateful boys and tall, wide-shouldered men with rippling muscles had nothing to do with Rose and her present dilemma.

A harried man glanced up from behind a brass cage and smiled.

"Morning, Ma'am. Come in on the Eastbound, did you?"

"I did." Rose smiled back. "Someone was to meet me, but it looks as if they've been delayed."

"Got family here?"

Judging by the eagerness in the stationmaster's eyes, Rose suspected her answer would be freely passed around.

"I do." She purposely didn't add more, mischievously enjoying herself. He'd have to dig for information, and Rose had no doubt he would. It didn't matter. She certainly had nothing to hide.

Curiosity won over the few seconds of silence. "And they'd be?"

"Who'd be?" she asked, innocently.

"Your family. You said you had family." Exasperation laced his words.

"I did, didn't I?"

The man sputtered, and Rose knew he thought she was either dumb as a stick or purposely avoiding his question.

"Ben and Wisteria McCabe," she answered, not a bit sorry for teasing him.

"Dr. Ben McCabe?" His pleased expression said it all. She nodded.

"Well, Ma'am, why didn't you say so?"

"I believe I just did."

The stationmaster coughed to hide his obvious impatience. "You say they were to meet you?"

"Yes, I telegraphed. They knew I'd be arriving today, Tuesday." She started to say more, then caught herself. "I'll just take a seat, I'm sure they'll be along soon."

"Doubt it."

"I beg your pardon?"

"Said I doubt it."

Rose tilted her head, and she felt the robin bounce precariously in the nest. The hat was ridiculous.

"And the reason would be?" Her back had stiffened, her chin came up, and she looked the man straight in the eye as her clipped words drilled him.

"Monday," he said succinctly, seeming pleased that now he was the one making her dig for answers.

"I don't see what Monday has to do with my question."

"Well, Ma'am, today is Monday and your family isn't expecting you until Tuesday." A grin spread under his skimpy mustache.

"Monday?" Rose repeated weakly. It couldn't be. How could she have made such a mistake? Her shoulders slumped.

"I imagine the doctor and his family are at the Harrison's barn raisin'. Most everyone is. Gonna be a big feed and dancing later. Doc's sure a part of the town. We're lucky to have him."

The man was a font of information, none of it an answer to her situation.

Rose cleared her throat. "Is it far?"

"To the Harrison's? Several miles. You weren't thinking of walking? That'd be crazy. Too far and too hot."

Exactly what she'd been thinking. "All right. How far to the schoolhouse?"

The stationmaster wrinkled his brow. "A few blocks. Why?"

"I'm the new teacher." She hated giving him more grist for his gossip mill. "I will be occupying the attached living quarters. If you could either direct me, or perhaps you could take me? I would sure appreciate it." She blinked hopefully, plastering a sweet smile on her lips.

"Too far to walk—" He leaned forward, peering at her fashionable boots. "—especially in that footwear. And I can't leave the station."

Rose sighed. Her recent inattention to the life swirling around her had landed her in this mess. If she'd been her normal self, it never would have happened. But, as Petunia would say, no use crying over spilt milk. Only this milk wasn't just spilt, it was soured and curdled.

"Say, Jesse, you could take her." The stationmaster looked past Rose.

She whirled around, surprised to see the same man who had only a few minutes ago been wrestling a trunk onto a wagon, a wagon large enough to take her and her baggage to the schoolhouse. Heat rose to her cheeks, knowing he had to have heard all of the conversation. Her teasing the stationmaster and her deflation as she was brought back down.

Still, relief flooded over her. "That's wonderful. If you could load my bags, we could be on our way."

"No."

"No?"

Not answering, Jesse brushed past her and placed a bill of lading in front of the stationmaster. Then he turned on his heel.

"Wait," Rose cried. "You can't just say no and leave me standing here."

He gave her a steely look, his hazel eyes narrowed as gold flecks darkened. He was handsome in a rugged, chiseled way. His prominent cheekbones hinted at Indian ancestry. And if the situation had been different, she would have found his face and broad shoulders worth a second look. A flicker flared in her heart. Ridiculous. The grim man standing in front of her could not possibly be the cause. He was abominable.

"Why?" he growled.

"I . . . I . . ."

"You're not my problem, lady. It's not my fault you don't know the days of the week. Schoolteacher—" he snorted.

"I do know the days of the week. And you are insufferably rude." She'd walk the few blocks, ridiculous boots or not. Blisters would be welcome compared to taking help from this-this man. "I don't need your help."

"Yes, you do," he said coldly and slammed the door behind him.

Chapter 3

Rose defied the stationmaster to say anything. If he so much as looked pleased, she'd reach through the cage bars and choke him.

"My bags are on the platform," she said, the words clipped. "I assume you'll see they come to no harm. Dr. McCabe will pick them up tomorrow." With that, she marched out the door.

Then she stopped short. The platform was empty. A headache that had been threatening now tightened her skull. Her bags were nowhere to be seen. She wanted to scream, *"What more? What possibly more?"*

"Get in," the voice growled from beside her.

Rose swirled around, coming face-to-face with the ruggedly handsome man. He was close enough she could smell his clean, masculine scent of pine, leather, and horse. Forgetting herself, she inhaled deeply.

"Look, lady, I don't have all day. You may have the luxury of standing there daydreaming, but I've got a ranch and chores waiting. Now, get in."

His curt words jarred her back to reality. Instead of being lost, her bags were stowed in the back of his wagon.

"Mr., uh, Mr.—"

"Rivers," he spat.

"Mr. Rivers." Rose drew herself up into all of her five foot three inches and tried to look him in the eye. "I have no intention of being indebted to you. I regret you took it upon yourself to load my bags into your wagon, but if you unload them, you can be on your way."

For just a second, his mouth quirked with amusement, admiration flickering in his eyes. Then it was gone, replaced with a cold glare.

With startling quickness, he spanned her narrow waist with his two large hands, picked her up, and plunked her down on the hard wagon seat.

Before she could sputter a word, Jesse rounded the wagon, seated himself beside her, and snapped the reins.

"Don't make me regret this anymore than I already do," he warned.

"I wouldn't think of it," she muttered.

He was a hateful bully of a man. And, he was raising a son just like him. Rose refused to look at Jesse and held on to her angry thoughts, embellishing them with relish the short distance to the schoolhouse. Short it might be in a wagon, but she admitted it would have been a long, painful walk. Well, it had been his choice, and she wasn't about to thank him.

Rose jumped down from the wagon the second it stopped in front of the red schoolhouse perched on a small hill overlooking the town. Fields of waving grass surrounded it, dissected by the banks of a winding creek. She was so caught up in the surroundings of her new home and place of employment that the bags were unloaded and Jesse was back in the wagon, snapping the reins before she became aware of his actions. He'd dumped her like unwelcome baggage.

"Mr. Rivers." But she was calling after a cloud of dust and a man's broad back as the wagon lumbered out of sight.

Rose muttered a few unladylike words under her breath and vowed she'd say them to Jesse River's face the next time she saw him. Her mouth twisted in concern as she scowled at the heavy bags by the schoolhouse step, squatting and waiting like fat, black beetles.

At least he got me here. I should be thankful of that. Now all I have to do is pray the school is unlocked. Then

I'll muster these infernal bags up the stairs and into my wonderful abode. Ha!

Jesse had no sooner rounded the corner than he regretted his actions. He should have carried her bags inside. Some of them were heavy and she was such a little bit of a thing. He stopped his thoughts right there. He wasn't about to dwell on how right she had felt in his hands. And it was only the hot sun that had caused his heart to pound.

Sure, he was anxious to get back to the ranch, but that wasn't the real reason for leaving the beautiful schoolmarm standing in the dust. No, it was because he knew if he didn't get away from her he'd do one of two things. He'd either kiss that saucy, red mouth of hers, or shake her until that absurd robin bounced off her head. He found himself smiling at the thoughts—both of them.

What was done was done. He just hoped she wouldn't be vindictive and hold his actions against Tory. The poor kid had enough troubles without his teacher taking her frustration out on him. He grinned, realizing Tory's size alone should intimidate the school lady. *If* he could force Tory to attend school enough days for it to even matter.

Tory had a grudge against the world. A valid grudge, but darn it, he'd done his best since coming back. Didn't the kid have an ounce of forgiveness in him?

Jesse knew the answer to that: No. Forgiveness would be a long time coming. Forgetting would be even longer. And the past was impossible to forget.

The day Jesse had left the Rocking R he'd turned his back on his little brother's pleas to not leave him. He'd hugged Tory and tried to explain he couldn't take a four-year-old along when he had no idea where he was going. He only knew that he had to escape his father's unreasonable, and often brutal, wrath before he reacted and did something—something he'd live to regret. The rage and beatings were happening more often, and they were turning him into a pain-filled fuse waiting to be lit. It could happen the next time meaty fists pummeled his body or the bullwhip was grabbed.

So, like a thief, he left in the night on a nag stolen from his father's barn. Rode out and left Tory crying in his bed, tears drying on his pinched face as he whimpered 'please' over and over. Jesse promised to come back just as soon as he'd made a place for the two of them. But the years tumbled one onto another, shaping him into the bitter, reclusive man he now was. Seven years of riding herd on someone else's cattle, seven years of long, dusty cattle drives. Seven years saving every penny earned, telling himself that he'd come back for Tory when he finally saved enough. Now he was faced with a growing boy filled with bitterness that rivaled his own.

Jesse shifted. Well, he was back, not because there was enough money, or even because he wanted to be back. No, his return was due to a letter from his stepmother that had finally caught up with him.

His own mother had died trying to give birth to yet another stillborn child. Touting he needed more help on the growing ranch, his father had turned a deaf ear to warnings that any further pregnancies could be fatal. Sons were the cheapest labor to be had. Wore down from miscarriages, his mother had simply given up. Then, without her there to take the brunt, *he* had become the focus of his father's drunken anger and cruelty.

His stepmother Emma's letter begged him to come back to the Rocking R. She was dying, and in paragraph after paragraph, she divulged that his father's wrath had turned on Tory not long after Jesse had left, and the boy had come to know the beatings and unending work. For the past seven years, he'd taken Jesse's place.

His father was dead, Emma wrote. He'd been drunk and tried to ride a green-broke horse. He'd been thrown, landing head first in a rock pile and never regained consciousness. At her death, Tory would be left with no one. She'd try to hang on until Jesse returned. The ranch, despite his father's drinking, was flourishing, and would be divided between the two boys. *"Please hurry,"* were her last words.

He had. But he hadn't been in time. Emma died two days before he arrived to face the brother he no longer knew. To face the brother that had learned at an early age to trust no one and to smother any feelings except those of anger and resentment.

A year had passed since Jesse had ridden into the empty ranch yard. After his mother's death, Tory had, with all the belligerence of a towering eleven-year-old boy, refused to stay with a neighbor and remained in the empty house. A house empty of love, but filled with grudging resentment.

Jesse shook off the memories as he drove the wagon to the barn and began unhitching the team. Tory was nowhere to be seen. The miles from town were nothing to the young boy. Not for the first time, Jesse felt the winter winds of loneliness sweep through him.

Chapter 4

Luck was with her, Rose thought. The schoolhouse wasn't locked. With a great deal of muttering and evil thoughts about tall, lanky, cowboys, she carried her bags up the steps, leaving them in the entry porch. In spite of herself, she was eager to explore where she'd now live and work. For the first time in weeks, the gloom gave way to a ray of hope and excitement. She ventured into the main room. Rows of desks in various sizes lined the room. Blackboards spread along one wall and a potbelly stove held court in one of the corners. In another corner a rope as thick as her fist hung from a hole in the ceiling.

Rose walked over and squinted up, then smiled as realization dawned on her. A bell was housed in the tall steeple. She could see herself pulling the rope to ring the eager students in at the start of the day, and later, from lunch recess.

She would wear her best black skirt and white ruffled blouse with the high neck and small pearl buttons marching down the front. Even though they pinched, she'd wear the fashionable boots with the high heels. After all, she was an example to the young girls and to the community. She would be a teacher to be proud of, one people would point out, marveling at the luck of having her teach in Wise River. Rose paused, pondering if she should wear her hair in a bun or braid it, wrapping them as a crown around her head. That decision would take more consideration.

There was no doubt the children would love her and would greet each day with smiling faces, calling out, "Good Morning, Miss Bush." Rose was grateful she'd taken back her maiden name. It would not have had the same, lilting sound for them to call out her married name, "Good Morning, Miss Mulligan." Her laughter bounced from the walls, hollow in the empty room.

Renewed by the whimsical musings, she continued around the room, stopping to pick up a book lying on a desk, or to tuck a ruler in the shelf under one desktop. Hers would be a tidy classroom, ready for parents or school board members at a moment's notice. Of course, she'd warn them that, while they were welcome, classwork must not be interrupted. An education was a serious matter, and she would brook no deviation from the learning experience.

Still caught up in her daydreams, Rose glided over to the teacher's desk at the front of the room and eased herself in the wooden chair. Scooting it closer, she folded her hands on the desk and scanned the room. As she did, unexpected waves of fear and cold realization assaulted her. All her fanciful wonderings flew out the schoolhouse door.

The reality was, she was no more a schoolteacher than a farmer's pig. She had no idea what to expect from her students and, worse yet, no idea what to expect from herself. She could plan what to wear, but she had no idea how to plan a lesson. In a few days, a classroom of boys and girls of all ages would look to her for knowledge. Not only that, but the school board would keep close tabs on the new teacher. Failure was imminent. Rose would fail, and in the process, she would lose the home provided her.

With a heavy sigh, Rose placed her palms on the desk and pressed up to her feet. Tilting her chin and summoning her courage, she opened the door and stepped into the adjoining room.

Sunlight streamed through sparkling windowpanes. The spacious room was inviting and clean. She held her breath, not daring to move for fear she would break the spell and this cheerful welcome was merely another figment of her vivid imagination.

But it wasn't. Her eyes were drawn to the round oak table with a lace tablecloth and a small jar of wildflowers in the center. A pleasant odor of beeswax and honeysuckle tickled her nose.

The kitchen range with its shiny, black top and two warming ovens, would surely heat the room, and if she left the door open, some of the classroom. It took no trick of the imagination to see the teakettle, now resting on the back of the stove, whistling merrily with hot water for tea. In fact, and she eyed the wood neatly stacked in a box beside the stove, a cup of tea would be heaven right now. As soon as she finished exploring, she'd bring in her bags and start a fire. Whoever had prepared this pleasing room wouldn't mind—after all, it was hers—at least for the time being. She smiled fondly at the beckoning rocker, snuggled near the stove.

Rose ran her hands over the cold stovetop and lifted the lid to the attached reservoir. With a fire going in the range, there would be hot water. A luxury for dishes, washings, and baths.

She drew back the heavy curtain separating the sleeping area. It was then Rose knew beyond a doubt that Wisteria had been the one who put the homey touches to her sister's new home.

Gently, she touched the familiar quilt gracing the inviting bed. Years ago, Petunia had made it for her and Wisteria. Rose had loved that quilt and wanted it for her very own. There had been grumbling and much arguing before the girls had agreed to share. Now, Wisteria had given it to her to enjoy. And the memories of two girls snuggled beneath it, giggling and sharing secrets, would be enjoyed, too.

"Thank you, Wisteria," Rose whispered, blinking back the tears filling her eyes.

Miraculously, all her earlier doubts left her, banished by the love-filled Morning Star quilt and the teakettle waiting to be filled. She could do this. She was a fighter. Anyone who could rope and drag a bawling calf out of a sucking mud bed could figure out a lesson plan. Today, she'd unpack and settle in. Tomorrow, she'd start the outline. Surely, the previous teacher had left some sort of curriculum.

Rose raised her arms and began removing the pins out of the firmly attached hat. Placing it gently on the bedside table, she began to free the coronet of braids. It was pure bliss to comb her fingers through her long, unbound hair, enjoying the freedom from the scalp-pricking hairpins and the heavy hat. Her traveling coat followed, as did the uncomfortable boots. A sigh of relief passed her lips. With determination, she placed one stocking-clad foot in front of the other and walked back through the waiting classroom to get her bags. Yes, tomorrow was another day. A challenge to be met and conquered.

Chapter 5

It seemed to Rose that she had just closed her eyes when a pounding on the schoolhouse door jerked her awake. Someone called her name.

Grabbing a duster, she stumbled through the rooms, and, recognizing the voice, threw open the door.

Wisteria pulled her forward in a fierce hug.

"I'm so sorry, Rose," she said breathlessly. "We thought you were coming today. Oh, how awful to arrive alone with no one to help you. Can you ever forgive me?" The apology bubbled out of Wisteria along with several more hugs.

"Silly goose. There's nothing to forgive. I got the days mixed up. Still, you could have left more than one loaf of your delicious anadama bread. Let's see if the range still has hot coals from where I banked it last night. I'll put on the teakettle. We'll have what I had for supper, tea, and the last few slices of bread."

"It's so good to have you here in Wise River." Wisteria's face clouded. "But I'm sorry you had to sell your homestead. You had such great plans." Wisteria took a seat at the table and watched her bustle about the room, shaking the stove grates, adding wood, and pulling the kettle to the front of the range.

"I'm not finished with those plans, Wisteria. This is just a bump in the road. I love ranching, and one day, someway, somehow, I'll have another chance. But for now —" She took in the inviting room. "—this is home. Because of you, I was welcomed. Your touch was everywhere." She raised her chin. "However, I must warn you. The quilt is now mine. All mine. It's not just a loan, is it?"

Wisteria laughed. "It's yours. But tell me, are your bags at the train station? Ben will be free later this afternoon and we can get them. He and that shadow of his are out doing house calls."

"Our precious Robin." Rose felt her heart warm. "She's still following Ben everywhere?"

"Yes. Still not letting him out of her sight, sitting quiet as a mouse while he's with a patient."

Rose shook her head. "There's no doubt she'll follow in his footsteps and be a doctor, too."

"Well, if not in Ben's footsteps, she'll follow her aunt Aries. If she's not out 'helping' Ben, she's out 'helping' Aries doctor. Poor mite, she hasn't a chance with two doctors in the family."

"Four years old. It doesn't seem right that her daddy isn't here to see her grow up. Though with the way Lee was turning out, it's for the best. You and Ben adopted her."

Wisteria smiled. "She was Ben's from the very beginning. And I quit thinking of myself as her aunt the first time she called me Mom. Actually, it was Momm, her own special way of saying the word."

"Well, you are the only mother she knows."

They fell silent, remembering.

Then Rose said, "To answer your question, no, I don't have any more bags. I was lucky enough to get a ride here, along with my bags."

"The stationmaster?"

"Nope, a good-looking man took pity on me." Rose loved the expression her teasing brought to Wisteria's face. "Good looking, arrogant, and not at all happy to be roped into assisting me. Brought me to the door, plopped the bags down, and took off."

"Did he tell you his name?"

"Jesse Rivers."

"Ahhh." Wisteria nodded. "He's not one of the more sociable people in Wise River. Wait until you meet his younger brother."

"I've already had that pleasure. I didn't actually meet him, but I was the recipient of a very disagreeable look. I don't think he and his brother get along."

"Tory doesn't get along with anyone. He is continually angry. I shouldn't be passing along gossip, but some things you need to know. Word is both he and Jesse were mistreated by their father. It was common knowledge the man used his fists on both of the boys. Jesse ran away years ago. I doubt he would have returned, but his stepmother wrote him she was dying and would be leaving Tory alone. Since he came back, Jesse has done wonders with the ranch. But I think he's having problems with Tory. Getting him to go to school is only one of many."

"Poor boy. Knowing this, I'll certainly have more understanding and patience with him." She smiled. "His handsome brother, too."

"Rose. You're incorrigible. Now, tell me, are you excited?"

"No. Scared to death. You know I've never taught before."

"Sure, but I also know you were always the best student. In fact, our last year of school, you spent most of the day helping the teacher teach."

"Oh, Wisteria." Rose took a bite of the flavorful bread. "I wish I had paid more attention to her lesson plans and class scheduling. I have a vague idea of how it's done, but to teach eight grades at one time runs shivers up my spine. Then throw in a couple unruly boys and whispering, giggly girls and . . ."

"You'll do just fine. Along with those shivers, a steel rod runs up your back. Once you make your mind up to something, you don't let anything, or anyone, stand in your way. Believe me, you are more self-reliant and better educated than the former teacher, Mr. Macon. He was a monster and a bully. He taught through intimidation."

"Well, I won't be a bully or intimidate. If there's a way to reach these students, I'll find it. And Mr. Rivers will be the brother he should be and see that Tory attends school."

"I have no doubt of that. Jarrett threatened Mr. Macon that if he ever took his rod to Timmy again, he'd come to school and break it over his head. The children were scared to death of him."

They both reached for the last slice of bread.

Grinning, Rose said, "Take it. But you do know the person taking the last piece has to replenish it."

"Ha! It's your recipe, Rose Bush. You're the bread maker. Mmmm, I remember your Christmas breads. Makes my mouth water. Just think, you'll be here for Christmas." Wisteria paused, giving her sister a hard look. "You will be here for Christmas, won't you, Rose? You aren't planning on leaving?"

"Not planning, no. But if . . ."

"No! There will be no 'but if's'. I just got you here and you owe it to me, to say nothing of the school board, to stay the full year. And more, if I have my way." Wisteria's uncharacteristic outburst filled the room.

Busying herself, not wanting to look Wisteria in the eye, Rose crossed over to the range. She poured more water from the merrily hissing teakettle into the chunky, brown teapot and set it down on the table to steep.

"It's getting warm in here," she said. "I think I'll open the door to the schoolroom and let some of this heat in there. I'll be working at that desk most of the day and . . ."

"Stop it, Rose. Your avoidance isn't going to work. Are you or are you not planning on staying the year at least?"

Rose sat down with a graceless thump. "Yes, I'm planning on staying the year, unless, oh, Wisteria, you know my heart's in ranching. The year I spent on my own homestead is one of my happiest memories. I've made several bad choices in my life, but buying that homestead wasn't one of them. I'm a rancher through and through." She scooted her chair closer to the table, wrapping her hands around the empty teacup, and said dreamily, "Waking up in the morning, smelling the fresh air, knowing that my day would be full. Knowing there were animals waiting, depending on me. My cow to be milked, chickens to be fed, eggs to gather, stalls to be cleaned . . . Yes, hard to believe, but I even didn't mind shoveling manure. Of course, I didn't enjoy the stink, or the cow smell in my hair from resting my head on the cow's rump while I milked. Ugh! The odor stayed in my nostrils all day."

"Rose, stop. You can't possibly expect me to believe you enjoyed . . .? No, that's not you. Not the Rose that loves pretty dresses and silly, impractical hats. Not the Rose that had every boy in school falling at her feet. The Rose that could have had her pick of men and yet chose, oh, I'm sorry"—Wisteria's hand flew to her mouth—"I shouldn't have said that."

"Yes, you should have. My marriage was a mistake. I fell for his fancy talk. His being so much older than me made him seem steady, dependable, someone I could rely on. How foolish I was. But one good thing came of that marriage, selling the house left me enough money to pay down on the homestead. Just not enough money to tide me through bad times," she said musingly. "I'll know better next time. And, Wisteria, there will be a next time. I'll wake up with the same excitement, anxious to start the long day of farming and ranching. Anxious to saddle my horse and check on my small herd. Next time, I'll have enough money to ride out anything nature throws my way. And I'll do it myself. I know you're happy with Ben, he's the love of your life. But

I don't need or want a man. All he'd do is force his ideas on me and stop me from doing anything he didn't feel was woman's work. No, I'll stay, but only long enough to save what I need. I'll stay, enjoy you, Ben, and little Robin. I'll be one of the best teachers Wise River ever had." Rose lowered her voice and her eyes. "But I'll not stay one minute longer."

Chapter 6

Rose rubbed at her sore neck, arched her stiff back, and again reviewed her copious notes. Grades kindergarten through eighth. In the school she had attended, one boy was older than the teacher. She had to smile at the remembered image of him towering over the diminutive Miss Prentis, his stumbling over words from the primary reader. Short in stature, no one got the best of the formidable teacher. Miss Alice Prentis could give you a look that would freeze your blood. Once was all it took, and big or small, everyone towed the line and learned.

Rose stared again at the former roll call book. She wished, not for the first time, the man had put the grade and age beside each child's name.

Twenty-five students. Too few books. She would have to approach the school board about that. In the meantime, she'd just have to figure her own way. And she would. Her earlier trepidation was vanishing, and darned if it wasn't being replaced with excitement. *Who would have thought it?* Rose curved her lips into a smile. She would conquer this mountain. And while conquering it, she would step day-by-day closer to her goal. Closer to having her own place, her own ranch.

Rose glanced at the pocket watch resting on her desk. She loved this little timepiece. A woman, down on her luck, had sold the watch to the mercantile in the town where Rose and her husband had lived. It had been pushed aside in the dusty case, as if waiting for her. Without batting an eye, she'd taken her grocery money and bought the watch. That act was fuel for one of her husband's more vituperative tongue-lashings. But it had been worth his every scathing word.

The watch was about the length of her thumb and could easily fit in the palm of her hand. She picked it up and pressed down on the round top of the winding stem, the case popped open, revealing Roman numeral numbers and the delicate hands keeping accurate time. Rose held the watch to her ear and smiled at the tic-tic of the watch's heart—a sound soothing and reassuring. The etchings of leaves and flowers on the outside cover nestled the barely visible initials, D.S. She'd given many thoughts to who this D.S. might be. She thumbed open the back and inner cover that protected the workings of the clock. There, engraved at the bottom of the cover, was an American flag and the timepiece's serial number. Manufactured in Elgin, Illinois. The owner had sold it for far less than it was worth, and she benefited from that poor sale. Even though it cost more than she should have parted with, she'd never regretted the purchase.

The rumbling of her empty stomach reminded her she'd had nothing but bread and tea for supper and bread and tea for breakfast.

She'd have to do some shopping but, bless Wisteria, the cupboards held enough to tide her over until she got her feet under her. And getting her feet in under her meant doing the necessary planning for school scheduled to start in two days.

With visions of a steaming bowl of the savory stew Wisteria had brought over, Rose made it as far as the entrance to her living quarters when several demanding pounds came on the outside door.

She crossed the room through the entry vestibule and opened the door, only to be confronted by three sober and unsmiling faces, two women and a man. The women were garbed in dresses of severe black bombazine more suitable for mourning than a social call. Equally mournful hats sat on tightly coiled hair, not one strand on either head dared to venture out of place. Their lips were tightly pursed lines. The lone man was cut from the same cloth of beady-eyed disapproval. All three wore a countenance that said the world was a bitter, unhappy place, and they were missionaries to see it stayed that way.

"Good morning, well"—Rose gave a nervous chuckle—"afternoon, I should say. May I help you?"

"You are Rose Bush?" The words snapped from the man's mouth.

"I am."

"Recently hired to bring education to the children of Wise River?"

"Yes." Rose frowned. Unconsciously, her back stiffened and up came her chin. Her eyes darkened as she met their censoring ones. She made no attempt to soften the flash of immediate dislike and resentment.

"We"—and he gestured to the two women—"constitute the Wise River School Board. We are here to instruct you on our rules and regulations as well as our clear expectations."

Before Rose could open her mouth, they swept past and marched through the small vestibule and into the classroom. Was it her imagination or had the sun taken refuge behind a cloud, deserting the previous sunny windows and leaving the panes bleak and cold?

"Sc-School board?" she stammered, trying to banish the apprehensive chill down her spine.

"Do you have a speech impediment, Miss Bush? If that is the case, you will be most unsuitable to educate our children."

"No." Rose took a deep breath, chiding herself for letting her uneasiness show. "I assure you, my speech is quite adequate. I suspect as adequate as yours, sir." She had to bite back the grin threatening to slip out at the man's horrified look. *Rose, don't you dare let the imp inside you get the upper hand and cause you to lose this job before it's even begun. Remember the money and the homestead it will buy.*

"My diction is not up for discussion, Miss Bush."

"Of course not. I apologize for my choice of words. Please, seat yourselves." She realized belatedly that the only seats in the room were for children. Momentarily, the ridiculous picture of the stiff, unbending people in front of her, squeezing behind a small desk threatened another giggle. What was the matter with her?

"Let me get chairs from my quarters. Please excuse me."

Rose made a hasty retreat, and once inside the sanctuary of her room, expelled her held breath. "Chairs," she muttered to herself. "Three chairs."

One-by-one, she carried the chairs into the classroom. No one offered to assist her. Clearly, she was the minion here, the recipient of suspicious scrutiny. Her role was to do their bidding.

"May I offer you a cup of tea?" Rose asked after the trio had settled themselves.

With stiff, erect carriages, the two women sat on the edge of their chairs, their posture perfect, spines at least three inches from the chair back. The third chair was left empty as the man had commandeered the one behind the teacher's desk and sat there with assumed ownership.

"This is not a social call, Miss Bush." He was obviously the spokesman for the formidable group.

"No, of course not," Rose said quietly, and at the wave of his hand, took the remaining chair.

As if on cue, the two women re-positioned their chairs to face Rose. Like a recalcitrant child, she'd been maneuvered into the undesirable position of three against one.

"I will make introductions. The lady on the left is Mrs. Chinney. Seated next to her is Mrs. Backley. And I am Mr. Whimpstutter." At each name, Rose received a curt nod from the recipient.

They fit their names. The unflattering comparisons hurled themselves through her mind. Mrs. Chinney had no chin. Her face seemed to end under thin lips. Apparently on the day the Good Lord was handing out chins, Mrs. Chinney was absent.

Mrs. Backley certainly had one, a quite large one in fact. Her ample backside stuck out behind her like an overstuffed bustle. And poor Mr. Whimpstutter was indeed a wimp of a man. It took no trick of the imagination to know he would use his position of authority to overshadow his skinny, short frame. He was a scrawny scarecrow with a pointed nose and jutting black eyebrows. His childhood must have been miserable, full of hateful teasing and bullying.

Rose blinked twice, hoping these dangerous thoughts didn't show on her face.

"I'm pleased to make your acquaintance." What a lie. She was anything but pleased and was sure she would be less so as the 'instructions' proceeded.

Mr. Whimpstutter reached inside his vest pocket and withdrew a folded sheaf of papers. Meticulously smoothing them flat on the desk, he adjusted his glasses and licked his fish puckered lips.

"Article Of Conduct," he read in a sonorous voice.

"You will not marry during the term of your contract. Keeping company with men is frowned upon and if believed unseemly, your position will be terminated.

"Your business in stores will be conducted with expediency and loitering or gossiping will not be condoned.

"Should you decide to do any traveling out of town, you must first obtain permission from the president of the board."

Mr. Whimpstutter cleared his throat. "That would be me, Miss Bush."

"Your dresses will be of subdued colors and will be the length of the top of your shoes. You will"—and a red blush crept up his sunken cheeks—*"wear two petticoats at all times.*

"Riding in a carriage with a man not related to you is forbidden."

"I believe we can make an exception here for Dr. McCabe. However it would be preferable that his wife be present."

"Quite," Mrs. Backley interjected.

"Indeed," Mrs. Chinney said.

With a satisfied nod, he continued. *"You must be in your living quarters during the evening hours unless you are attending a school or church function.*

"You are expected to keep the classroom clean and ready for inspection at all times. Lamps are to be filled and chimneys cleaned daily. Fresh water is to be carried in by you and the two buckets filled daily. It is your responsibility to see that there is sufficient wood stacked for each day's use.

"Men teachers may court, taking only one evening a week to do so. They may also take one evening a week to attend church services."

"This, of course, does not apply to you, Miss Rose."

Rose found herself speechless, relieved that no response was expected.

"You will be frugal with your pay, setting aside savings for your aging years. Society will not want you as a burden.

"After your eight to ten hours in the classroom, you will spend the remaining evening grading papers, preparing for the next day's classes, reading your Bible, or suitable, approved books of good works.

"Your performance will be reviewed during weekly inspections. After a time period of at least five years, and if your performance has been acceptable, a raise of fifteen cents per week will be given. The school board will vote to determine if you are worthy of this increase."

"Do you have any questions, Miss Bush?" Not waiting for an answer, he shuffled his papers and said, "Good, let us continue. These are a few of the most pertinent rules of conduct for your students. You will be expected to adhere strictly to them."

"Talking among students and in the classroom is forbidden unless absolutely necessary. Remember, children are to be seen, not heard. Disruption to classmates is also forbidden and infraction will result in punishment handed out by the teacher. Obedience and acceptance of punishment is expected.

"Fighting, name-calling, rude noises, or spitting, is not tolerated. The Golden Rule will be practiced at all times.

"No fidgeting, whining, or crying is permitted. Children will sit upright on benches or behind their desks. There will be no slouching.

"Hats or caps will be removed upon entering the classroom.

"The teacher will inspect each child for cleanliness. Attention will be given to clothing, ears, necks, and in general a clean, pleasant-smelling body. This will be done each day prior to the start of class.

"Clothing for both boys and girls will cover the extremities completely. No young lady will show a bare ankle."

"Now, we will go over the punishments."

"Punishments?" Rose asked weakly.

Mr. Whimpstutters eyebrows rose at her daring interruption.

"Punishments," he reiterated in a severe tone.

"Spare the rod and spoil the child," Mrs. Chinney said.

Three heads nodded emphatically.

"We will continue," Mr. Whimpstutter said.

"The rod will be used with firmness and often."

"If a student is tardy, he or she will remain after school for one hour."

"This is a right-handed world. A child favoring their left hand will receive one whack with the rod."

"Should a child speak without being prior spoken to by the teacher, or if they talk in class, they will receive 1 whack with the rod.

"Unruly behavior will not be tolerated. Should this behavior occur, the guilty party, or parties, will receive six whacks each with the rod.

"Chewing or spitting tobacco is forbidden. It is the devil's weed. This will result in eight whacks with the rod.

"Profanity or immoral language will never be tolerated and will result in immediate suspension from the school. This will be followed by a meeting with the child's parents.

"ATTENDING WISE RIVER SCHOOL IS A PRIVILEGE. UNACCEPTABLE, ILL-MANNERED CHILDREN WILL NOT BE GRANTED ENTRANCE TO THE CLASSROOM." His voice boomed out the final words.

"Whacks? Rod?" The words caught in Rose's throat.

Mr. Whimpstutter peered over the top of his glasses at Rose.

"Whacks," he repeated loudly. "The rod will be used often and with exuberance. Miss Bush, I've had my doubts a woman has the ability or strength to dispense discipline as necessary. Do you have that ability?"

But before she could answer, Jesse Rivers barged into the room, carrying an armload of wood. Making as much noise as possible, he dumped it into the woodbox next to the stove. Then, casting a brief look in Rose's direction, he gave her a conspiratorial nod.

For several minutes he'd stood unseen in the entryway and heard the rules being laid down, he'd also heard the bullying of Mr. Whimpstutter. Disgust had filled him at the unfairness of the situation and the man's belligerence. An interruption had been called for. He quietly returned to his wagon and proceeded to fill his arms with wood.

Originally, he'd entered the building intending to ask Rose where she'd like the wood stacked. He hadn't made it any farther than the vestibule when anger filled him hearing the three browbeat her with their narrow-minded rules and demands. He didn't recall making the decision, he just knew she needed rescuing.

"Mr. Rivers, you are intruding. Is this necessary?" Mr. Whimpstutter sputtered.

"It sure is. I furnish the wood for the school, and I deliver it when I have time. Do you have a problem with that?"

The three were speechless. Rose noted that Jesse Rivers had only to enter a room to own it.

"Now if you'll excuse us," Jess continued, "Miss Bush and I have to decide where to stack this wagon load. I'm sure that if you leave your rules behind, she will be quite capable of reading them."

"Well, I never." Mrs. Chinney started to protest only to clamp her mouth shut at one quelling look from Jesse.

Muttering and harrumphing, their chins pointed upward, the trio indignantly marched out the door.

"There will be weekly inspections," Mr. Whimpstutter threw back over his shoulder, determined to have the last word.

"She'll be ready," Jesse muttered.

Chapter 7

"Mr. Rivers, I—"

"Sit down, Miss Bush, before you fall down. I don't plan on catching a woman indulging in vapors."

His words had the desired effect. The earlier anger fueled by the edicts of the school board, coupled with Jesse's brusque command, flared into life. Her face took back her rich color and twin spots of displeasure rested becomingly on her cheeks. Her nostrils expelled air filled with fire and warning. The warning was lost on Jesse as he recognized and applauded the fighting spirit of the woman facing him, hands on each hip.

"Don't you dare presume to tell me what to do. I am not anyone's doormat."

Jesse shrugged. "Could have fooled me. You were doing a darned good imitation while Mr. Whimpstutter read you the rules of conduct."

"Rules of conduct," Rose snorted. "Well, here's what I think of their rules of conduct." She marched to the desk, grabbed up the papers, and threw them into the air. A feeling of satisfaction filled her as she watched the papers flutter and fall. Her rosy lips curled into a wide smile that made Jesse's heart do a curious flip.

"Hmm," he muttered, enjoying baiting this feisty woman. "Maybe you do have the ability and strength to give out whacks with the rod."

"There will be no whacks or rod in my classroom," Rose fumed as she paced in front of the desk, missing the imp in Jesse's eyes. "I may want, no, *need* this job, but I won't be bullied into acting outside my principles. Spare the rod and spoil the child. Ha!" She narrowed her eyes, drilling them into Jesse. "I won't be dictated to by you either, Mr. Rivers. While I may owe you thanks for your timely interruption, that's all I owe you."

"It wasn't timely. It was planned."

"Planned?"

"Yes."

"How much did you hear during your eavesdropping?"

"Enough. Enough that I knew if someone didn't interrupt and stop you, that fiery temper you were trying to hold in check might erupt and there would go your teaching job before it even started."

"Why do you care?"

"Oh, I don't care. Not about you or your job. That's your problem. And, from what I'm hearing you say, you don't have any great love for teaching." He held up his hand to stop her protests. "Like I said, I don't care. What I do care is seeing that Tory gets an education. And it appears you have been elected. Wise River has been without a teacher too long. Those three dragons guarding the schoolroom have found reasons to refuse every applicant. You have Ben McCabe and his influence in this community to thank for your job."

Jesse felt cruel as he watched some of the fight leave Rose. He shouldn't have thrown all that in her face. Not after her brush with the school board. Still, he wasn't about to be swayed by eyes with depth and color that changed with her every mood. He had to be cold, immune to her courage and spirit. Immune to any woman.

Rose took a deep breath. As much as she hated to admit it, she already knew that having this position was because of Dr. Ben McCabe. It was a bitter pill to swallow, knowing this was one of the rare times she hadn't been in total control of her life. And, it appeared, others saw that, too.

"Mr. Rivers, how or why I got the position is something I won't discuss. However, I will concede I'm not here because of any great desire to teach. It is not my first love. But"—she cast him a warning glance—"I will deny that with great vehemence, should you desire to blab what I've just shared." She shook her head, her eyes never leaving his.

She continued. "I am committed to teaching the boys and girls of Wise River. Not with a rod but with patient forbearance and recognition of what constitutes being a child. I am qualified to teach. And, you can put your mind to rest, Tory will receive an opportunity to learn. Now, I'm sure you have better things to do than stand here. I'm grateful for your timely interruption. Thank you. I do need this job and you are correct, my tongue would have lost it for me. You may put the wood wherever you think best." And with a swish of her skirts, she flounced out of the room.

"Well, I'll be damned. Hate to admit it, Jesse, but that little wisp of a woman put you in your place and told you what for." Chuckling to himself, he went out to his wagon and load of wood with a surprisingly light step. Teacher Rose Bush would be someone to watch, and maybe every now and then, to bait.

Rose slid back the curtain from the kitchen window, and hiding behind it, watched Jesse unload the wood. She'd seen muscular, handsome men before, but there was something about Jesse Rivers that captured her attention. *It certainly isn't his sweet disposition. Still, I have to give him credit for acting quickly in what was about to become a tense situation. And just because I admire his physique and good looks doesn't mean I'm not aware that a snarly disposition inhabits that body.*

Then, not giving herself time to question her actions, she slid the coffee pot to the front of the stove and reached for two cups. Removing the glass dome from the cake plate, she cut a large slice of the tiered chocolate cake she'd baked earlier and placed it on a saucer. Taking a deep breath, Rose opened the back door and called out, "Mr. Rivers."

Jesse leaned against the now empty wagon and wiped his brow with a bandana. He eyed the stacked wood with satisfaction. It wasn't enough, but it would last a few of the cold winter months. He'd bring more before the snow fell.

"Mr. Rivers," Rose called louder.

Jesse turned and again forced back the fluttery feeling in his stomach. She was an attractive woman. That's all it was. Well, hell, she was beautiful, not merely attractive.

"Yes?" he said, his voice curt.

Rose caught back the smile on her face, already regretting her impulsive decision to invite this arrogant man into her home. Darn. Oh well, she'd finish what she'd started.

"Would you care for a cup of coffee?"

"No."

"Fine." She flung the word at him. And before he could say anything, she slammed the door.

He couldn't resist. He ambled over, cracked open the door, and called into the quiet kitchen, "But I'd sure welcome a cold glass of water."

Rose whirled, her hands on her hips, mouth pursed, ready to do battle. But Jesse wasn't looking at her. He was staring at the large slice of chocolate cake resting by an empty cup. His mouth watered as he looked up. "Mine?"

"It was. Now I'm not so sure."

"I am." He winked at her, and with a small dimple dancing at the corner of his mouth, he slid into the empty chair and picked up the fork.

Rose glared, then took her frustration out on the hand pump on the sink, grabbing a glass and vigorously pumping it full of cold water. The indoor pump was a luxury, one she wished was also present in the classroom. Toting buckets of water was a job she didn't look forward to.

She plunked the glass down so hard, some sloshed over the side.

"Thanks." He pretended not to notice her hot temper, and drained the glass. "Now I'll take that coffee."

"Coffee?" she spluttered.

"Sure. Goes real good with cake. You bake this?"

"Of course I did, Mr. Rivers. It didn't just sprout up and grow in this kitchen."

Jesse took a large bite and let the rich chocolate roll around in his mouth. "Mmmm, mmmm. Ma'am, you ever get tired of teaching, you could open a bakery. I don't believe I've ever tasted cake as good as this."

Jesse's words of honest praise defused Rose's temper. Filling both cups, Rose gingerly took a seat across from him. Oblivious to her, he took one bite after another, concentrating only on the quickly diminishing cake. Giving a sigh, he regretfully took the last bite then scraped his fork across the empty plate and brought it to his mouth, giving it a lingering lick.

"More?"

"Sure. But I won't." Embarrassed, he remembered his manners. "Aren't you joining me?"

"I had a piece earlier. I take it chocolate cake is a favorite of yours?"

"Teacher Bush, anything I don't have to cook or burn trying to cook is a favorite of mine."

Rose laughed, surprised by his wit and the enjoyment she felt in his presence.

"Not a cook, huh?"

"Nope. Not even. Tory tries and between the two of us, we don't starve."

"I'll cut a piece for you to take home to him, and if you don't make me angry again, I'll include a second piece for you."

"You've got a deal. But since your fuse is mighty short—"

"And your tongue is mighty sharp," Rose interjected.

Jesse threw back his head and laughed. He'd done more smiling and laughing in this woman's presence than he'd done in a mighty long time. She was infuriating, that was for sure. But she also proved a delightful opponent.

Chapter 8

Jesse was still smiling when he pulled the empty wagon into the yard. His quick assessment took in the quiet ranch and too-empty house. It would be nice if just once Tory was there to meet him. Hell, it would be nice if just once Tory wasn't wearing a scowl on his face. He'd take anything. Any overture of friendliness would be an improvement. How was he ever going to reach this brother who had become such a resentful, distrusting stranger?

Looping the reins over the wagon brake, Jesse ambled over to the barn and opened the wide doors. Tory turned, and seeing Jesse, a mask shuttered his face. He moved in front of a wooden box, hiding it in a secretive manner.

"I didn't expect you back," he snarled.

"I live here, Tory."

"I know you do. I just meant— Never mind." He bent to pick up the box, making sure he covered it with his body, and started past Jesse.

Jesse reached out and touched the boy's arm only to have him jerk away as though he'd been touched by a red-hot poker.

Jesse's hand fell to his side as feelings of hopelessness rushed through him. "I, uh, I brought you something."

"Yeah, what?" Tory asked suspiciously.

Jesse walked back to the wagon and returned, holding out the plate of Rose's cake.

Tory's eyes lit up and a hint of a smile caught the corners of his mouth. There it froze, as if the muscles had forgotten how to move in any direction other than a frown.

"Where'd you get that?" his brother asked.

"From the new schoolteacher." Jesse grinned, pushing the dish toward Tory. "She sent you a piece."

"Why?"

Jesse's grin faded. "I don't know why, Tory." His voice filled with exasperation. "Does there have to be a reason for everything?" As soon as the words were out of his mouth, he regretted them. It was too late. He'd just given Tory the opening he'd been waiting for.

Tory's hand flew out and he knocked the cake to the ground. "Here's a reason for you," he growled. "Try I don't want it." He whirled around and ran out of the yard into the thick copse of trees surrounding the back of the ranch.

Jesse's first impulse was to go after him, grab him by the shoulder, and shake some sense into the brat. But that was what Tory would expect. What he'd received for longer than Jesse cared to admit.

He bent down and carefully picked up the cake where it had flown from the plate, landing on a patch of weeds. Jesse turned it over in his large palm. Clean, well sort of, and he brushed a couple leaves from the rich chocolate. A dab of icing stuck to his finger and he stuck it in his mouth, sucking off the sweetness. Placing the cake back on the plate, he moseyed toward the house. If Tory refused to eat it, then he would. Darned if he'd let a perfectly good piece of cake go to waste.

Later, as he unharnessed the team and went about the rest of the never-ending chores, his mind went over the eventful day. Tory hadn't returned to the house. Sometimes he spent the night in the woods, more at home there than at the ranch. "And around me," Jesse muttered.

He'd tried giving Tory time and the privacy the boy seemed to demand. But it wasn't working. Tory threw off every overture Jesse made. Maybe he'd been wrong not to call him on some of his actions. Like the cake. Anger once again filled him and he wanted to take off into the woods, see what the allure was that called to his brother. But he didn't and wouldn't.

He carried an armful of split wood into the kitchen and started a fire in the large range. Filling the coffee pot, Jesse couldn't help remembering an earlier cup and the warm hominess of a kitchen filled with a woman's presence.

His eyes roved over the large farm kitchen, comparing it to the small room attached to the classroom. The entire living area would come close to fitting in this one room.

Jesse's father hadn't scrimped when it came to something he wanted. And a large house was something he'd wanted. Four bedrooms, a spacious living room, a good sized kitchen with a mudroom entry, and an office, made up the two-story house with the wraparound porch.

Jesse made a derisive sound. The living room was a joke. The lavishly furnished room fooled one into imagining pleasant evenings gathered in front of the river rock fireplace. There had been no pleasant gatherings. In fact, Jesse couldn't remember the four of them being in that room at the same time. The fireplace was rarely used, and the stiff and uncomfortable furniture was for show only.

What he could remember was his mother, and then his step-mother, silently shuffling from room to room, fighting the unending dust, keeping the house as spotless as his father demanded. Two of the bedrooms were shut off and never used. Although there were two boys, they weren't allowed rooms of their own. Now, Jesse occupied the room that had been his parents', and Tory remained in the bedroom they'd shared once long ago.

Returning home, the first thing Jesse had done was to strip the bedroom and get rid of the furniture. He'd raided one of the unused bedrooms for a bed, dresser, and chair. But before he'd moved in, he made a trip to town and came home with a large tin of the new Sherwin-Williams paint.

It was only after the paint had refreshed the room, making it his, had Jesse moved in. There were still times, though, when he'd catch himself looking over his shoulder, expecting to hear his father's heavy footsteps in the hall.

Jesse shook the grates in the cook stove and set a cast-iron skillet over one of the lids. Another supper of fried steak, gravy, and too-hard biscuits. That it was filling was the highest praise that could be given.

He took his time and, knowing it was useless, set two plates on the table. Slowly drinking his coffee, Jesse waited. The gravy thickened and a skim had layered over it when he said to hell with it. He dished up his meal, eating it while glaring at the empty place facing him.

After the last dirty dish had been washed and the skillet scoured, Jesse climbed the stairs to his room. He paused outside the closed door of Tory's empty room. The showdown he'd been putting off was looming closer. There had to be rules set and one of them would be Tory would attend school. Eleven years, going on twelve, and he still could only read primers. Whatever allure the woods offered, school, helping around the ranch, and being present for meals, would be priorities. Jesse blew out the lamp, and the last thought he had before sleep claimed him was that tomorrow he'd lay down the law to Tory Rivers. A promise that filled him with trepidation.

A promise that would have to wait. By morning, Tory still hadn't made an appearance, and once again, Jesse started the day with a solitary meal, but a smile quirked his lips. Tory had been back sometime during the night. The now-empty cake plate sat in the middle of the table.

Chapter 9

Rose rubbed her tired eyes and drew the shawl tighter around her shoulders. She leaned against the kitchen doorway enjoying the sweet morning air breathe softly against her face. It carried a hint of autumn, and Rose gave an involuntary shiver at the thought of winter coupled with the cold Montana wind.

She squinted into the early morning gray, barely able to make out the wood stacked neatly against the shed. Although it was only a few feet to the pile, it would be a miserable job gathering the frozen, snow-packed wood and carrying it into the schoolhouse. She hadn't explored the shed, but maybe it could be cleaned and Jesse River's next load of wood stored there. Yes, that's what she'd do today.

Today, the last day before school started. The last day before everyone in Wise River, Montana knew what a failure she was as a teacher. The last day before she'd have to face a class of upturned faces, waiting for her to . . . To what? Teach them? Impart knowledge to them? *Oh, Rose, what a foolish mistake you've made.*

She'd made several trips to Ben and Wisteria's home determined to tell them she would be moving on and wouldn't be Wise River's teacher. Surely they would understand and not want her to stay and be humiliated. But each time, she'd retraced her steps back to the schoolhouse, lacking courage to even knock on their door. Where was the Rose of old? She missed her. Each time, she'd returned to the teacher's desk and reviewed her lesson plan, re-working it until the page was a mass of illegible smudges.

Rose took another breath and let a smile creep across her face as she thought back to Jesse sitting at her kitchen table, wolfing down cake. He'd even let his guard down long enough to share a few stories about the cattle drives, the men he'd worked with, and the country he'd seen. Yet when Rose had asked him if he regretted leaving that behind and returning to Wise River, he'd shortly replied, "No." The dark look on his face advised her not to pursue that line of questioning.

She'd mentioned Tory and couldn't help but notice the tense, worried frown that crossed Jesse's face. He didn't disclose much, mentioning only that Tory had problems reading. She had tried not to let her surprise show when he said Tory was unable to read higher than the beginning primers. Piecing together more from what he didn't say, she surmised Tory fought him over everything, attending school included. Jesse Rivers was a man carrying the weight of the world on his broad shoulders. She had such an urge to reach out and help. Why she would want to share the burdens of a man she'd just met and wasn't sure she even liked, was something better left alone.

"He's had a hard twelve years," Jesse said. "Now I'm back, and he has to adjust to having me take over and tell him what to do. And, to make matters worse, he's shot up bigger than most of his friends. That is," he'd muttered under his breath, "if he has any friends."

Jesse had gone on to assure her he'd step in if Tory gave her any trouble. Just thinking about it made Rose shiver.

The sky in the east was losing the night's grip, and a sliver of pink mixed in with shades of gray heralded the promise of sunrise. Rose took one last lingering look and stepped back inside.

She had an agenda. Today she'd clean the shed and make sure every chore in her meager domain was caught up. Keeping busy might stop her mind from scattering every which way.

Several hours later, there was an empty shed and a pile of trash to show for her efforts. Finishing that task, she'd heated water and done the washing. Her back ached, but it was a good ache, one born of a job well done.

Rose bent over the oven door and removed a pan of corn bread. That, and the honey Wisteria had left, would make her supper. After she ate, she'd carry in the washtub and fill it with hot water from the stove's reservoir. A warm bath, clean sheets, and a tasty supper should make for a good night's rest. Shouldn't it?

But it didn't. The sheets twisted around her legs as she tossed and turned. Finally, with a disgusted mutter, she threw off the covers and limped to the kitchen table. Fumbling in the dark, she removed the chimney from the kerosene lamp resting there. What a blessing to have a kerosene lamp. Kerosene was costly, so she had to use it sparingly, but she loved it.

Carefully placing it back in the center of the table, she closed her eyes, letting the brief peace brought about by the welcoming glow of this lamp fill her. Its light cheered the center of the room, driving the night shadows back to hide in corners and against the walls.

Rose took two steps away from the table, took another step, then stopped. "Oh, my," she said, her eyes as wide as the grin on her face.

Turning around, she went to the lamp and hesitantly placed her palms around its warm base. Perfect. It was perfect. Here in her kitchen, in her hands, rested not only the class's first history lesson, but also their first art project.

Muttering the word "perfect," Rose dropped into a chair, her mind whirling with possibilities and plans. She would teach *her* way, not someone else's, and certainly not by the rigid rules set down by the school board. She'd always done things her way, confident and ready to meet any task head on. She wouldn't confine herself to books. Absolutely not. She'd bring everyday objects alive for the children. Her guide would be the familiar items making up their world. The possibilities were endless. Didn't she already have a history and art project and the day hadn't even begun? She could do this. Of course she could. Energy coursed through her. Energy and excitement.

Begrudging the time spent coaxing the kitchen range into life and filling the coffee pot, Rose hurried back to the table eager to map out each step of the glorious idea.

As she planned, waves of gratefulness filled her. Wisteria and Ben had encouraged the townspeople to donate any books. Surprisingly, several textbooks and four McGuffey Readers were offered. Aries, Ben's sister-in-law and a doctor, had generously given several of her father's reference and history books. She and Jarrett also gave several Big Chief tablets purchased from the mercantile. Rose would keep them at her desk and judiciously hand out the paper for special projects. And, making it nothing short of a miracle, the school board had loosened purse strings and provided chalk and slates for each child. Wise River was making every effort to assist her in educating their children.

Grateful that worry had robbed her from sleeping, Rose rejoiced now that she had hours before school would start. The time would be put to use assembling today's first lesson. She could hardly wait. The thrill of anticipation was new and strong enough to banish any earlier fears.

She gulped down her breakfast of oven toast and coffee. Then she grabbed a bowl and mixed up a batch of cookies. *I'll have a snack ready each day. Most of the children are from outlying ranches and will have started their days early with chores waiting to be accomplished. Perhaps I'll make cooking another lesson to be taught.* She laughed at the idea. *No, most of the girls could prepare a meal at an early age. They could probably teach me a thing or two. That's it! Cooking can be another area to explore. The boys can take the topic of fire and . . .* Her mind was off as possibilities jostled each other. And if an errant thought broke through of wishing she was starting the day on her own ranch with cows to milk, chickens to feed, eggs to gather, and a myriad of other chores waiting to be completed, it was quickly banished to the back of her mind. It would wait there along with the errant thought of Jesse Rivers and his rare smile.

Chapter 10

Rose grabbed the rope and gave it a tug. The school bell rang out clear and strong, a carillon of sound winging over the small town. Standing by her desk, Rose waited for the children to arrive. After several minutes, a tight knot formed in her stomach. No one had arrived. Grimly, she marched over to the bell and just as she was about to give the rope another tug, the sound of feet shuffling across the vestibule's floor and the subdued sound of children's voices reached her. She breathed a sigh of relief.

The children filed in, sober faced, with all signs of happiness or excitement missing. Like little soldiers, they marched to individual desks, and staring straight ahead, arms stiff at their sides, stood beside them. Rose watched them, puzzled at first, then realization broke. They were taking the same seats assigned to them by the last teacher. She stared at each face, hoping to see a smile, or to even hear a "hello." There was no sound in the room except for a few restless feet.

"Good morning." Rose was relieved her voice wasn't trembling. "I'm Miss Bush, and I'm your new teacher." She waited for a reply. None came. "My first name is Rose and if you put my first and last name together, you'll find it makes the silly name of Rose Bush. She forced a smile. "That will be easy for you to remember, won't it?"

"Yes, Miss Bush," the class chorused without a trace of emotion.

Now what? "Well, uh, Good Morning. Oh, I already said that." She ran her tongue nervously over her lips. "Are you standing at your assigned seats?"

"Yes, Miss Bush."

"Well, then, please sit down." No response. "You may be seated," she said more loudly.

Silently, moving as one, the children fell into their seats. Rose noted two little girls had remained standing.

"Don't you have an assigned seat?"

Their little heads shook. The girls couldn't have been much older than three.

"Are you new?"

"Yes," one lisped.

"Does anyone know anything about these two girls?"

Silence met her question. Then tentatively a hand rose.

"Yes." Rose nodded, relieved.

"They are my sisters. They're twins. Ma said they were old enough to come to school now."

"Their names?"

"Sarah and Lucy."

"Sarah and Lucy," Rose repeated. "And their last names?"

"Trawley."

Rose glanced down at her roll call book and saw the name Amanda Trawley.

"You must be Amanda."

"Yes, Miss Bush." Again, the monotone response. Rose felt sure that by the day's end, the words "Yes, Miss Bush" would be enough to make her cringe.

Just then the door flew open and hit against the wall. Tory Rivers stood scowling in the doorway. Not saying one word, he marched to the corner in the back of the room and stiffly stood there.

Rose's eyes widened as she watched his blustery entrance. What on earth? She was totally at a loss to explain his actions.

"Tory," she called out to the boy grimly standing in the corner. Like the other students, he had adopted the earlier pose of body erect, arms stiffly at his side. "Please take your seat."

A few subdued snickers greeted her request.

Tory didn't respond, his posture rigid, his eyes focused on a space somewhere behind her head.

Rose raised her voice. "Tory, please take your seat."

Still no response. Tory wrinkled his brow. Reluctantly, his eyes dropped, meeting hers with a puzzled expression.

Amanda's hand snaked up.

"Yes, Amanda." It would seem that having suffered no consequence from her earlier experience, she was the self-appointed spokesperson. She had dared to raise her hand without the teacher requesting her to do so.

"That is his seat, Miss Bush. Well, it's not exactly a seat." Her voice dropped off.

"The corner?" Dumbfounded, the question fell from her lips. "Standing in the corner is his seat?"

"Yes, Miss Bush," Amanda answered.

"But . . . but that's not a seat. It's a corner," Rose said, stating the obvious.

She looked at Tory for an explanation, but other than the flush now working its way up his face, there was no response. Then she glanced back at Amanda.

Emboldened, Amanda said, "That's where he stays. Mr. Macon said he was a dunce and had to stay in the dunce's corner. Mr. Macon said he was a big dummy. Mr. Macon said—"

"That will be enough, Amanda."

It was as if a cold wind had filled the room, freezing every set of eyes in her direction. Rose gripped the edge of her desk while her mind raced for a solution. Anger was slowly filling her. How dare someone subject a young boy to such-such humiliation? Her eyes flashed and she bit her lip to keep from voicing the thoughts clamoring inside her head. She'd love to get her hands on . . . No matter. There was a bigger problem facing her than the former teacher.

Where would she sit a boy much too big for the remaining empty desks? If Tory tried to squeeze into one of them, his knees would touch his chin.

A problem that had to be resolved immediately. And Rose felt the way she resolved it would set a tone in her classroom. One that would be lasting. She was being judged by twenty-two sets of eyes.

"Very well. Here's what we're going to do. I need two blocks of wood, about the same thickness. Would one of you boys volunteer to go out to the woodpile and bring them in?"

The children looked at each other. Finally, one of the older boys stood up. "I will, Miss Bush."

"And your name is?"

"Art. Art Mackey."

"Fine. Thank you, Art. And Timmy"—she smiled at Timmy McCabe, her sister's new nephew—"would you help?"

There wasn't a sound in the room as Rose and the students waited for their return. All faces had shifted to the door and no one wished for a speedy return more than Rose.

Finally, they appeared, each carrying a thick block of wood.

"Thank you." She tapped one of the empty desks. "I will need both of you boys to take hold of a side of this desk. When I give the word, you will raise the desk and hold it in place while I slide a block under each runner. Can you do that?"

Heads nodded.

"All right. Get ready. Lift!"

The desk raised and in minutes the wood was in place. And while it looked ungainly, it was now high enough to accommodate a tall boy, knees and all.

"Thank you, boys. You've been a big help."

Tentative smiles acknowledged her thanks.

"Tory, this will be your seat from now on. Please try it out. If it isn't accommodating enough for your remarkable"—she emphasized the word, letting it hover in the room—"height, then we'll just look for thicker blocks. I apologize. I should have had your desk ready. My brother was a tall as you and that's how his teacher solved the problem.

Tory's mouth fell open in surprise. He couldn't have moved if he'd wanted to. She was apologizing to him? She called his height remarkable? Not sure if he heard her right, he remained rooted to the floor until Miss Rose wiggled her fingers, smiled, and motioned him forward.

Shoulders hunched, he dragged his feet to the altered desk and silently slid into the seat. It fit. His feet rested on the floor and the top of the desk was waist high. Just like everyone else's. He had to fight the urge to smile.

"Does it feel comfortable, Tory?"

Tory swallowed hard. And in a scratchy voice replied, "Yes, Miss Bush."

Chapter 11

Jesse cursed as the hammer missed the nail and hit the edge of his thumb. He gave the nail another whack and stood back. The corral was a heck of a lot sturdier than when he'd started.

The morning had been seven kinds of hell from the moment he'd yelled Tory awake to when he'd delivered him—sullen, angry, and late—to the schoolhouse door. He'd had the wagon hitched and ready to go, so being late wasn't his fault. It was because Tory deliberately dawdled with everything Jesse had asked him to do. Tossing hay to the horses was drug out until he'd lost patience and jerked the pitchfork out of Tory's hand and finished the job himself.

Tory couldn't be trusted to walk the few miles to school. Jesse had learned that the hard way. It had taken a visit to the former schoolteacher questioning why Tory's hands were red and swollen from being smacked with a ruler, and why he wore marks of the teacher's rod, only to be told Tory was absent from school more than he was present. And, according to Mr. Macon, when he was there, he was rude and a behavior problem. In short, Tory was a troublemaker.

Tory hadn't mentioned any of this, nor had he complained about the teacher's brutal treatment. In fact, if Jesse hadn't noticed the grimace on the boy's face when he gingerly lowered himself to the kitchen chair, he would never have questioned the arrogant teacher. Coupled with that, his gut told him Tory was lying when he claimed his hands were the result of trying to grab a trout laying in the cold creek. And when he finally did, Jesse felt ashamed. He'd got so caught up in the responsibilities of the Rocking R, he'd forgot about the real reason he'd come back—Tory. He'd let the memories and pain lurking, ready to pounce the moment he'd rode onto his father's ranch land, takeover and win.

It had been all Jesse could do not to use the cane on that insufferable bully. As it was, he'd grabbed the teacher by the front of his shirt and shook him until his head darned near snapped from his skinny neck. They probably heard him all the way to the feed store when he'd roared out what he'd personally do should a cane or ruler ever be used on Tory again.

But none of that solved the problem. Tory hated school. And while Jesse didn't blame him, he knew Tory had to have what education Wise River could offer. So he'd taken on the added chore of hitching the wagon and delivering him to the school each morning. And now if he lingered in the schoolyard it was for no other reason than to make sure Tory was securely inside the building.

Like a litany, he reminded himself that those actions, that rage, was evidence there could never be a woman or children of his own in his life. He didn't dare. He was his father's son. And if he doubted that his father's blood coursed through him, all he had to do was recall how hard it had been to stop with merely shaking the cane-wielding teacher. He'd had to fight himself not to beat the man senseless with his fists. Even now all he had to do was close his eyes and see the red welts across Tory's buttocks and lower part of his back to have blinding rage fill him. Rage similar to what his father had displayed time after time for any infraction of the rules. Rage that had been handed down from father to son.

He didn't think he'd ever strike a woman or a child. But he didn't know that for sure. It had sickened him to see his father take out his wrath on his stepmother. He'd felt so helpless, especially when the man had turned on him. Jesse felt sure it was this same behavior that had hastened his mother's death, killing her will to live. He'd been too young to know what was happening or to do anything about it. Then when he was old enough to stand up to the violent man and offer some protection to his stepmother, what had he done? He took the coward's way out and left. Didn't that action make him as guilty as his father for the abuse Tory had then been subjected to? He'd let down a child that had always looked up to his older brother.

No, he'd never marry and take the chance. He didn't dare allow any remorse for this decision to affect his life.

Jesse gathered his tools. His stomach rumbled, reminding him he'd skipped lunch. Because of Tory's dawdling, he hadn't taken the time to do more than grab a cold biscuit for breakfast. Time to start the evening meal. He'd eat and do more chores before falling into bed once more so tired he ached. Still, there was satisfaction in working the land again, a sense of accomplishment. Now if only Tory would come around. A sigh fell from his lips, and emptiness filled him.

Tory should be getting home from school soon. Maybe if he worded the questions just right, he'd get him to open up, share his day. Heck, he might even hear how the new schoolmarm was doing. *I've every right to be curious. I'm only looking out for my brother.*

Jesse dreaded each day, knowing Tory would defy him over anything he could. It seemed as if his brother was determined to make him pay the rest of his life for his earlier decisions.

He ignored the ache in his back. There wasn't time to brood over his minor pains. Tomorrow had every promise of being another busy day. He'd promised Jarrett McCabe, on the Big Horn Valley Ranch, he'd help put a new roof on a hail-damaged shed. Jarrett was not only a neighbor, but they had become friends since Jesse's return, often giving each other a helping hand. He knew full well Jarrett was

Wisteria's brother-in-law and knew also that Wisteria was
Rose Bush's sister. The information had no special meaning
he assured himself. Just an interesting fact.

Jesse shifted the cast-iron skillet to the back of the stove
and gave a disgusted look at the bacon curling in the pan.
He'd attempted pancakes and bacon, knowing this had once
been a favorite meal of Tory's. It had been a waste of effort.
Dusk had fallen and he wasn't home yet. Supper was ruined.
Again. Jesse knew he wasn't that great of a cook anyway.
His meals were monotonous, and more often than not, he'd
burn something. But they were worse when eaten cold.

He curbed down the resentment felt for the absent boy
and grabbed a plate off the shelf. He'd eat. Grabbing a cold
pancake, he spread some butter over it and took a bite. Jesse
made himself chew and swallow the lumpy mess. It was
food of sorts and he was hungry.

Emma had been an excellent cook. Thoughts of her
Sunday fried chicken still made his mouth water. He'd tried
frying one of the hens too old to lay. It had been a disaster
start to finish. He hadn't realized feathers soaked in hot
water, ready for plucking, could smell so bad. Still, that
smell wasn't anything compared to what had whooshed out
the minute he'd inserted his knife into the hen's stomach
for gutting. He'd about lost his breakfast when he grabbed
the warm entrails and yanked them free. The cut-up pieces
frying in the pan looked nothing like Emma's. In fact, they
looked nothing like parts of a chicken. The wings and back
were one large piece. He couldn't find the joint to cut and
separate the thighs from the legs. So he'd just hacked and
guessed, resulting in the bare knob of joint protruding from
the top of the leg.

Burnt on the outside, raw on the inside, neither he nor
Tory could eat it. The disgust in Tory's eyes said it all. He'd

shoved his plate across the table and stalked out of the kitchen—just another night he hadn't returned to the house.

Just then, the sound of a door slamming open jarred through the kitchen followed by heavy treads across the wooden floor, heading toward the stairs.

"Tory," Jesse called.

There was no response save for the halted steps.

"Tory, come in here. Now."

Jesse held himself still. Surely Tory wouldn't defy him so openly. Minutes ticked by while Jesse stared at the doorway.

"What do you want?" The words preceded his brother's glowering face as Tory sauntered into the kitchen.

"Where have you been?"

"Out."

Jesse felt his patience slowly ebb from his body. "Out where?" He spit out the question through clenched jaws.

Tory turned on his heel and started out of the room, ignoring Jesse's last question.

"Tory, don't you dare walk out of this room. Get back in here and *sit down*!" he said, each word a bitten command.

A red flush rose up Tory's face as he whirled around and grabbed a chair from the table. He slammed his body down, slouching in the chair as though anything his brother might want or say was of no consequence to him.

"Supper is ruined."

"Yeah." Tory's lip curled. "Like it was worth eating anyway."

Jesse bit back an angry retort. "I'm not a cook. But damn, darn it, I try."

Tory snorted and focused on the kitchen window as if his eyes could penetrate the gathering darkness.

Jesse tried another tact. "How was school?"

"Okay."

"Look. I know this is hard—"

"You don't know anything."

"Tory," he said in a warning snarl.

"What?" Tory gave him a look that was both bravado and fear. "You gonna show me how big and strong you are, maybe take a rod to me like—"

Jesse only heard the word rod and he jumped to his feet, sending his chair backward.

"What do you mean rod? Like who? Did that new schoolmarm take a rod to you?" He rounded the table and grabbed Tory by the shirt, giving him a shake. "Huh, did she?"

"No, she spent the day blabbing about stupid rules." Tory jerked out of his grasp and tore out of the room. His final words drifted back. "Look, I don't need you. Why don't you just leave? Just leave."

Chapter 12

Rose sipped her tea and smiled to herself. The first day of school was over. She was exhausted, but it had been a success. Well, sort of a success. The children seemed excited to learn, and if they had to be coaxed to join in discussions, that was understandable. Actually, it had taken all of her talent and patience to get them to participate. Fear of discipline reigned. The specter of the former teacher floated throughout the classroom, reminding them of all the rules of discipline, especially. *Should a child speak without being prior spoken to by the teacher, or if they talk in class, they will receive one whack with the rod.*

After several fearful glances at the rod, Rose had slowly walked over to the offending object, and accompanied by gasps, grabbed it, faced the class, and said, "There will be no use of the rod in my classroom." She marched over to the outer vestibule and deposited it behind the door out of sight.

"However," she addressed the class on return, "I will expect perfect behavior out of all of you at all times. If I don't receive this behavior, I will contact your parents and they may use the rod as they determine fit." Not one set of eyes left her face. Then slowly, face-by-face, child by child, smiles grew. "Do you understand?"

"Yes, Miss Rose," they chorused.

"Fine. Now let's define our own classroom rules."

Some of the smiles faded. It had been too good to be true. Miss Bush was going to have harsh rules just like every other teacher.

"Art, do you have good penmanship?"

Art warily nodded.

"Then please go to the chalkboard and write the rules as the class tells you." She handed a piece of chalk to the puzzled boy.

Turning, Rose noticed a hand wavering from a desk in the middle of the room.

"Yes, your name please. You will all have to give me your names for the next few days until I know who you are."

The slight boy got to his feet, his head tilted until his nose was in the air and his narrow shoulders military erect.

"Willy, Ma'am. Willy Backley," he said, his voice a squeaky whine. "My mother is Mrs. Backley and she is on the school board."

Rose gulped. It was to be expected. That's what can happen if you become too prideful. She had been sure she was on the right track. Then she caught the superior expression on Willy's narrow face. He sensed her apprehension. That was all Rose needed to strengthen her backbone.

"Yes, Willy. You have a rule?" she asked hopefully.

"No, Ma'am. I just think you should know that my mother, uh, the school board, will not be pleased that you threw out the rod. My mother says we are to be raised up Godly and the bible says—"

"I'm quite aware what the bible says. Now, Willy, if you have nothing further to add, such as a rule, other than use of the rod," she hastily added, "then please be seated."

Rose turned her back to the class, choosing to ignore the snickers as Willy slowly sat back in his seat. Wrapped up in the skinny frame of one weasely little boy was trouble.

"Okay, class, let's give Art something to write. How about Rule Number One being 'A student may raise their hand in participation at any time?'"

This was met by vigorous nods.

And like a dam breaking, hands rose until the chalkboard was full. Rose handed out coveted sheets of paper from one of the Big Chief tablets and said the rules were to be copied using their very best penmanship, then handed in for a grade.

Thus flew the morning. The history of kerosene was tabled until tomorrow.

"Time is up. Those of you who have completed copying the rules may break for lunch." Her gaze roamed the room. "I will need a monitor." Rose hurried to explain. "This person will be chosen weekly and will be my second-in-command." Pleased murmurs greeted her words. "They will be dependable, trustworthy, and most of all, they will be kind. They will see that the younger children are looked after. They will see that there is no bullying on the playground. I will assign their duties each day. Now, who would like to volunteer to be our very first monitor?"

Several hands shot up. The former reticence seemed to have been placed alongside the vanquished rod.

"Thank you, all of you, for volunteering." She paused. "This week's monitor will be Amanda. I assure you, each one of you will have the opportunity to be monitor before the school year ends. Are there any of you that have not finished copying the rules?" Out of the corner of her eye, Rose noticed Tory's paper held only a few lines and several rubbed-out words. Words rubbed out so hard, small holes had appeared in their place. She would not embarrass this boy. She gathered his paper along with the rest. It was obvious Tory would need individual attention. But whether he would accept it was another matter.

Two little hands rose. Rose smiled. The three-year-old Trawley twins. She had given them some butcher paper and asked they draw a picture of their family. Of course they couldn't copy the rules.

"After lunch I would like one of our older students to sit with Sarah and Lucy and help start them learning the alphabet." Again hands waved. Rose basked in the excited participation. In one morning, the class had sprung alive.

Their enthusiasm was contagious. All caught it except Willy. His eyes were narrowed and Rose just knew he was committing to memory every infraction, every flaunting of a rule, and every new idea she introduced. That there would be trouble there was no doubt.

Rose directed the newly appointed monitor to lead the class to the playground where they would spend their lunch hour.

"Enjoy your lunches and the fresh air. When you return to the classroom, we'll have individual reading so I can ascertain your level and where you stand in this ability."

Rose missed the panicky look that crossed Tory's face as he lowered his eyes and followed the monitor out of the classroom.

When class resumed, Tory wasn't among the students present. The large desk was glaringly empty.

"Amanda, did you line up all the students?"

"Yes, Ma'am. Just like you told me. Soon as you rang the bell, we made a line and came inside." The small girl waited expectantly.

"Good job. You are making a fine monitor."

Like a flower opening to the warm rays of the sun, Amanda's face bloomed with pleasure.

"Thank you, Miss Bush."

Rose walked to the front of the room and stood in front of Tory's empty desk. "Does anyone know where Tory is?"

No one answered.

Rose tried another tactic. "Amanda, as monitor, you were watching the playground. Do you know where Tory is?" Rose gulped down the fear threatening to take over. On her first day she had lost a child. Not only that, but the lost child was Jesse River's brother. How could she face him and explain she'd allowed his brother to-to what? Disappear?

"Amanda?"

Amanda sighed and said resignedly, "Tory left. He always does. He never stays all day."

"Never?"

"No, Ma'am. Tory hates school. He only comes because his brother makes him. He used to not come in the mornings, but now he has to because his brother brings him to the door."

"I see." She didn't, but those were the only words she could think to say. Judging from the problem with the desk, Tory's banishment to a corner, and being labeled a dummy, she could understand only too well his not wanting to come to school under Mr. Macon's rod wielding rules. But hadn't she solved this? Hadn't she shown him that was a thing of the past?

"Does anyone know where Tory goes when he leaves here?"

Timmy raised his hand, and at Rose's nod, he said, "Tory goes to the woods. He stays there all the time."

"Thank you, Timmy and Amanda." Resolutely, she picked up a book from the desk. She'd just been handed another problem on her too full plate. A problem best shoved aside for another day. Perhaps tomorrow would be different. Perhaps tomorrow Tory would stay the day. Yes, and perhaps cows would fly.

Putting a smile on her face, Rose said, "Now, let's start our reading time. Who would like to go first?"

Chapter 13

Saturday, blessed Saturday. Rose shifted in the bed, stretching her body, reveling in the fact that today she needn't be up preparing for another day in the classroom. Today, she could lie in bed and do nothing. She could go for a long walk, she could borrow Wisteria's horse and buggy and go for a drive, maybe even a picnic, she could—the list was endless.

Laying there, she reviewed the past week. It had been a week of small successes. Mid-week, she had introduced her plan of bringing alive the history of everyday objects, starting with the kerosene lamp.

"Students," she said to the waiting class. "Do you know what this is?"

"Sure," one of the boys replied. "A lamp."

"Yes, you're partially right. But what kind of lamp is it?"

Heads turned, seeking the answer from each other.

Rose gave the class several minutes and when nothing came forth, she said, "It's a kerosene lamp."

Several grins followed the pronouncement. "We knew that, Miss Bush. We just thought you had some special kinda lamp there."

"Well, it is special. We have the luxury of the kerosene lamp because of Mr. Abraham Gesner. Mr. Gesner distilled coal and produced a clear liquid. Mr., or we should say Dr. Gesner, was both a geologist and medical doctor." Rose hesitated before continuing. There wasn't a sound in the room. Even Tory was giving her his full attention.

"Dr. Gesner poured the liquid into an oil lamp with an absorbent wick. He then lit the lamp and guess what?"

A hand in the back of the room rose.

"Yes?"

"The lamp worked?"

"It sure did. It gave off a beautiful, pale yellow flame. He named the liquid kerosene, which means wax oil. Some of you may know it by another name—coal oil."

Heads nodded and hands shot up.

"I know all about coal oil. Once my dad cut his hand, and he put coal oil in the cut."

"What happened?"

"The cut healed," the boy said importantly.

"My grandma uses it for her arthritis. She mixes it with fat then rubs it on. It sure stinks."

"I'll bet it does," Rose laughed.

"Yeah," another voice piped up, "and you can mix fat and coal oil together, tie it in a dishtowel, and then wrap that around your throat. 'Course you get big red blisters if you leave it on too long."

The enthusiasm was infectious as child after child raised their hand and contributed. All except Willy. He appeared totally disinterested.

"Ma makes us take a lick of molasses to coat our tongue. Then we wash down a spoonful of kerosene."

"Whatever for?" Rose couldn't keep the alarm out of her voice.

"Throat infection."

The home remedies seemed endless. The students weren't the only ones that had learned something today.

"Please clear off your desks and let's get ready for an art project. Oil lanterns were used many, many years ago in temples."

Willy's hand shot up.

"You shouldn't be telling us about them things, Miss Bush. God wouldn't like us talking about heathen religions."

God, or your mother? But to Willy, they were probably one and the same.

"Willy, I hear your concern, but I intend to continue with the lesson. Thank you for your input."

Rose swallowed the lump in her throat. There was no doubt Willy would rush home and tattle to his mother about Miss Bush's blasphemous lesson.

"Today, we're going to make Chinese lanterns." Rose took down one of the books from a pine shelf. Opening it, she passed around the picture of a glowing Chinese lantern.

"You will have to share the scissors, so let's work in teams of four. I've made a paste of flour and water. No eating it," she admonished, making her face stern. "When finished, we will hang the lanterns around the classroom. I'll give each team some material to be cut into decorations. Because they are flammable, we won't be able to put candles in them so be creative, use your imagination."

For the rest of the morning, Rose was kept hopping from team to team as paper was cut into strips, edges glued together, handles added, and material cut into imaginative designs and glued onto the paper.

Laughter and banter echoed as each team had no doubt their lantern was the best.

Rose gave a worried glance at Willy who had refused to join any team, stating he wasn't going to make something heathens used. He sat at his desk, head bent over a book, oblivious to the laughter and happy chatter.

But Tory's participation wiped out any disappointment felt by Willy's superior attitude. His ideas were sound, and before long, the other three on his team acknowledged him as the unclaimed leader. Tory was an artist and flower after flower was drawn on the material to be cut out and pasted on their lantern. Rose recognized several of the flowers having seen them growing in yards and in the countryside. The details were exceptional.

However, her pleasure was short-lived. Again, after the lunch break, Tory's desk was empty. She'd been so sure he'd return since experiencing overwhelming success and acceptance. His team's lantern was quickly acclaimed the best. Was there nothing that could reach this withdrawn boy?

That question was still buzzing around in Rose's head when she swung her legs off the bed. The question of what to do on this fine Saturday was settled. She'd borrow Wisteria's buggy and go on a picnic. She would not spend the day brooding over the past week. There had been no repercussion from the school board, so maybe Willy's tattling fell on deaf ears.

Don't be foolish, Rose. Mrs. Backley will believe every word Willy tells her. It's only a matter of time and the school board will come calling. So today will be a fun day. A day of relaxation. A day free from worries. A day to drive in the country and enjoy the sweet smelling air, but most of all, to enjoy my freedom. I've proven I can teach. This past week was evidence of that. But it still isn't what I want to do with my life.

Rose bustled about the kitchen, slicing bread and smearing it with elderberry jam. She poured some lemonade in a jar, then grabbed a handful of cookies and wrapped them and the bread in a dishtowel. Then she chuckled at her assembled lunch. Bread, jam, and cookies. Perfect.

The sun was warm on Rose's back as she stepped down from the buggy and looped the reins around the brake handle. She grabbed the lunch from the wagon seat, reached in under it for the jar of lemonade, and jauntily took off for the beckoning woods. A straw hat, decorated with a spray of pansies bobbed on her head.

As she entered the shaded woods, peace embraced her. This was a perfect idea, a perfect way to spend Saturday. And if she felt a niggling of guilt for not being at home planning next week's lessons, she quickly shoved it away.

So intent was she on looking for the ideal spot for her picnic, she almost missed the flutter of movement and the quiet voice riding the slight breeze. Rose paused, then stealthily tiptoed forward.

Crouched at the base of a large tree was a boy, gently brushing back pine needles and dirt as he murmured pleasure at whatever lay beneath them. Rose stretched her neck, but couldn't see anything.

She must have made a sound for he jumped to his feet and whirled around, facing her.

Tory.

He glared at her and shifted his body so as to hide whatever he'd unearthed.

"I-I'm sorry, Tory. I didn't mean to startle you."

"What do you want?" His lip curled as he bit out each word.

"Why, nothing. I don't want anything. I'm on a picnic and—"

Rose's words died. Tory's expression was unrelenting.

"These are my woods," he said defiantly.

Rose bent her head. "Really? Well"—she held up her food-filled hands—"this is my picnic. If you would be willing to share your woods, I would be willing to share my picnic."

Conflicting emotions ran across his face.

"I have molasses cookies," she offered. "Molasses cookies and lemonade."

"Guess I could," he mumbled. "But watch where you're stepping." With that, he moved to the side revealing a patch of delicate flowers crouched at the base of the tree. Each tiny bloom perfect in varying shades of pink and purple.

"Wood violets." Rose moved toward them. "They're beautiful. So tiny and perfect. How on earth did you know where to look for them? They're rarely seen." Whispering, Rose crouched down in front of the flowers.

Tory knelt beside her, his earlier animosity forgotten.

"They're also called Prairie Blue Violets," Rose said. "I have a cream pitcher with them painted on it. See their leaves"—she gently touched one delicate leaf with the tip of her finger—"they're shaped like a heart. They love moist or wet areas. That's why they're snuggled against the base of this tree where the dirt is shaded from the sun and remains moist."

"How do you know so much?" There was a tinge of earlier resentment in the question.

"I read. There're books on plants, Tory."

"Wouldn't matter." He shrugged and looked away. "I'm too dumb to read."

Chapter 14

Jesse squinted in the afternoon sun, questioning his decision to see what allure the woods had for Tory. The sound of voices filtered through the leaves, muffled by the oak brush and pines. He crept toward them, stopping short when hearing a woman's angry voice.

"Tory, I have a lot of patience, but I have absolutely no patience for remarks of that sort. You are not dumb. Do I have to yell those words at you to get you to believe them?"

Jesse carefully parted the brush hiding him and saw Rose with her hands on her hips, her face inches away from Tory's.

"Answer me, Tory," she demanded.

"What do you want me to say?" Tory demanded. "You want me to say I'm not dumb? Well, I won't say it, Miss Bush. I am dumb. I'm one of the oldest boys in the classroom, and I can't read as well as the younger kids. So what do you say to that?" he asked belligerently, daring her to respond.

"I'd say that's mighty convenient for you."

"Huh?"

"I said that's mighty convenient for you. You can miss school, only come when your brother drops you off, leave at the first opportunity, then whine that you're dumb."

He glared at her. "I don't whine."

"No? Well, what do you call it?"

"Telling the truth," he snarled.

Rose ignored the hurt in his eyes. If making Tory mad was the only way to reach him, so be it.

"Truth." She gave a false laugh. "Well, maybe I'm wrong."

Tory's eyebrows rose.

"Yes, maybe you are right. You're dumb."

"Told ya."

"Hiding out here in the woods, afraid to face people. Afraid of the classroom."

"I am not afraid," he bellowed.

Jesse tensed. Rose had gone too far. He started forward to make his presence known, only to freeze at Tory's next words.

"I don't hide out," he said softer.

"What?" Rose leaned toward him.

"I said I don't hide out."

"No? Then what do you do all afternoon when you're not in school learning to read?" she taunted.

Tory didn't answer.

Rose let the silence stretch between them.

Jesse held his breath. Should he step forward, end this inquisition?

As if having reached a major decision, Tory pressed his lips together and reached for a canvas bag lying to the side of the tree.

"Here." He thrust the bag at Rose.

Rose's fingers were trembling as she reached into the bag and drew out several sheaths of paper.

She glanced at them, then at Tory, her eyes widening with each page.

Flowers. Intricately drawn flowers. Front, backs, side views, every detail perfection. At the bottom of each page was a name—Star, Bell, Sun—simple names depicting the likeness.

"You drew these?" Rose asked quietly.

Tory nodded. His eyes searched hers, as if fearfully awaiting the verdict. "Most of them grow here in the woods."

"I don't know what to say."

Shoulders hunched, he made to grab them from her hands. "Give 'em back. I shouldn't have showed them to you. You probably think—"

"I probably think these are beautiful. I've only seen such meticulous drawings in a botany book." Slowly, she rifled through the papers, randomly pausing, murmuring praise as her finger gently traced a flower's outline.

Rose lowered herself to the ground. "Sit down, Tory. I've a picnic to share and"—she smiled at his drawings—"we've got a few decisions to make."

"Yeah, like what?" Tentatively he sat opposite her, a protective expression on his face for the papers she held firmly in her hand.

"Like how you and I are going to proceed from here. And how we'll begin private reading lessons." She handed him a slice of bread and jam. "In fact, we'll begin tomorrow."

"Tomorrow's Sunday," he said derisively.

"Yes, and that's what makes it a perfect day to start.

"I got work to do. Chores."

"I'll talk to your brother."

"Don't do that!" he exploded. "I don't want him to know. You can't tell him. He'll be mad 'cause I've been leaving school. Besides, he'll think I'm a sissy, spending my time drawing flowers. If you tell him, I'll tear 'em to pieces. The rest, too."

"You've more?"

He shrugged. "A box full. Ma saw that I had paper. She helped me hide them from my pa. But I will, I'll tear them up, I swear."

"We've a problem, Tory. I won't lie to your brother. If he asks me about school, I'll have to tell him the truth. Of course, if you started staying until school is dismissed for the day, well then I wouldn't have anything to tell, would I?"

Jesse almost wished he hadn't come upon the two. He had thought forcing Tory to attend school would solve the reading problem. He had no idea Tory stayed only long enough to sneak away. Why hadn't he looked deeper?

Flowers? Drawing flowers? He wouldn't pretend to understand. Ranching was all Jesse knew. It was something he loved. And being part owner in the Rocking R made all the hard work worthwhile. But flowers? Why would a boy want to spend his time hiding in the woods, drawing flowers, even if the drawings were as good as the pretty teacher thought? Jesse put aside the questions. It didn't matter why. If it brought any measure of happiness to Tory, then he would help his brother in any way he could.

The voices continued.

"I won't stay and read with the babies. You can't make me."

"Of course you won't."

"Huh?"

"We'll have private reading lessons until you can read as well as others your age. But you have to attend school all day. Either that, or I'll have a visit with your brother."

"That's cheating."

"No, it's not. It's trading. I'll trade you silence, and you'll trade me learning to read and attending school."

"Don't see how it'll work," he mumbled around another bite of bread.

"Leave that to me. We'll start our lessons tomorrow. You can tell Jesse that I've made a special request for you to help me with a project. That won't be lying. It is a project. A project to help a future botanist learn to read."

"A botanist? You keep using that name. Don't know what it is," he mumbled.

"It's what you are, Tory. A botanist is a person who studies plants, their life and growth. They also classify plants, that is, they learn their Latin names and sometimes even get to name a plant."

"A botanist." He let the word slowly roll from his tongue. Then he raised his head and gave Rose one of the first smiles she had ever seen on his face.

"You think I could be one?"

"I think you are one. Of course, you'll need further education. And"—she grinned—"you'll have to be able to read about the plants."

He nodded, his eyes alive with excitement. "You-you think I can?" Doubt filled his words.

"I know you can. I won't tell you the real names of the flowers you've drawn, but I have a book that will. You'll have to read it for yourself."

"Miss Rose"—he squared his shoulders—"you've got a trade." And he held out a sticky hand.

Chapter 15

Jesse noiselessly backed away from the conspirators. And for the rest of the day, their conversation buzzed in his head. He threw himself into his chores, wondering how he'd face Tory without revealing his secret. Anger, unexpected and fiery, whipped through him at the schoolteacher. Who did she think she was to invade his life this way? That he was being unreasonable didn't matter. What did was the fact she had entered into a deal with his brother. A deal that excluded him. Interfering spinster. Not enough schoolwork to keep her occupied, she had to meddle where it's none of her business. He'd be the one to work with Tory. He'd be the one to mend any fences, draw the boy out. He slammed the lid back down on the cook stove and grabbed a skillet and placed it on the range. Cutting thick strips of bacon from a slab he'd brought in from the smokehouse, he carefully laid them in the pan then poured himself a cup of coffee.

He stalked over to the window and looked out across the barnyard and to the woods beyond. Absently sipping the coffee, the anger rolled from his shoulders. The tranquility that entered every time he paused to let the surroundings engulf him brought a smile to his face. This was his ranch. Every building, every fence, every field bore his signature. From childhood up he'd contributed, and now it was his. He felt no sense of loss knowing his father would no longer be a part of the Rocking R. If he felt anything at all, it was relief. A smile teased at his mouth. The old man would be reeling in his grave knowing Jesse now called the shots.

A movement at the edge of the woods caught his eye. Tory. He was slowly crossing the fields toward the house, moving as if the weight of the world was on his small shoulders.

In a flash, Jesse knew he dared not reveal anything he'd overheard. As much as it galled him, he had to admit the nosey teacher had gotten more out of Tory in a few minutes than he'd been able to in a year. He'd play along but he'd be watching every step of the way. The minute she stepped out of line, he'd be there. It wouldn't matter to him how pretty she was or how cute her turned-up nose was, he'd mince no words letting her know Tory had an older brother quite capable of taking care of any of his needs.

The door opened, and Jesse turned toward the sound. He'd forgotten to prepare himself for Tory's habitual scowl. The look on the boy's face struck him in his chest with its coldness. He wanted nothing more than to cross the floor and pull the boy to him but he did no more than give him a nod.

"Supper'll be ready shortly. Wash up."

"I'm not hungry."

"You should be. You haven't had anything since breakfast. Have you?" Jesse couldn't help probing, knowing Tory had shared Teacher Bush's picnic.

"I, uh, I found something to eat in the woods."

"Oh yeah? Snared yourself a rabbit maybe?" Jesse taunted.

"So what if I did. You're not the only one that can take care of yourself."

"Didn't say I was." Jesse wished he could start all over and not push at Tory. He turned his attention to the bacon sizzling in the pan.

"Thought I'd crack a few of the fresh eggs I got from the Watson's. We'll have breakfast for supper. Then if you'd agree, I'd like for us to take a look at that pinto, see if you think he'd make you a good saddle horse.

Jesse's back was turned so he missed the way Tory's face lit up. For a few short minutes, he'd forgotten to hate.

"You . . . you mean it? I mean, sure if that's what you want, guess I can make time."

"Well, he'll take work. He's been let go until he thinks he's the boss. You'll have to show him who is."

"No!"

"What?" Jesse jerked around.

"I won't show him who's the boss. Not ever. If it means having to whip him into doing what I want—"

Jesse crossed the floor in seconds. "Tory, stop." He grabbed the shaking boy. "Now you listen to me. Have you ever seen me take a whip to a horse? Huh?"

Tory looked everywhere but at him.

"Answer me, Tory."

"No."

"Well then, why would I expect you to? I'd be darned mad if I saw you take a whip to any animal. You don't beat a horse into submission or to show him who's the boss. Just like you don't do it with family." He lowered his voice but didn't take his hands from Tory's shoulders.

"Our dad's way isn't mine," he said softly. "And it isn't yours. We've both been at the wrong end of being shown who's the boss, right?"

After a long pause, Tory nodded. "Yeah."

"Okay, then. From now on, we talk things out. You don't like something I'm doing, you tell me. I'll do the same with you. Nobody's the boss in this house. We're a team, partners. Joint owners in this ranch. I don't know about you, but I'm hungry, partner."

Jesse busied himself with the eggs, choosing not to notice the tears in Tory's eyes.

"Guess I could eat something. Just don't fry them like rocks."

"Runny?" Jesse asked.

"Not runny either. Here, let me." Tory shoved him aside and took the spatula out of his hand. "Ma taught me to cook some. After he died, it was just her and me. There were days she stayed in bed all day, sick."

"I'm sorry, Tory. I should have been here."

"Nothing you could have done."

"No. But that's no excuse for me not being around." Jesse walked back over to the window and looked unseeingly into the gathering dusk. "Do you think someday you and I could talk? Man to man?"

Silence greeted Jesse's words. Silence broken only by the scrape of the spatula in the hot grease.

Jesse felt his shoulders sag. Well, he'd tried.

Then a voice broke the quiet. A voice so low Jesse thought he'd imagined the words. "Partners to partners?"

Jesse tried to answer, but he couldn't move past the lump in his throat. He couldn't turn around either. He blinked hard and swallowed. A smile of hope creased his face and the weight on his shoulders took wings.

Chapter 16

Montana was experiencing a rare but beautiful Indian summer. October was creeping by and the classroom was resplendent with red and gold autumn leaves glued to paper, hanging from every available space. They'd had an afternoon nature hike with Tory leading the class and returned with handfuls of leaves dressed in autumn finery.

True to their bargain, Tory had attended school each day, all day, never disappearing in the afternoon. Granted, his face wore a frown most of the time and he rarely participated. But when the day ended, Rose saw a different boy emerge. They'd leave the classroom and go into her inviting kitchen where she always had a snack waiting. Then, sitting at her table, they'd tackle reading. In a few weeks, the primer was relegated to the bookshelf and McGuffey's First Eclectic Reader appeared. They worked on the alphabet, then graduated to the script alphabet. Tory had the handwriting of an artist.

Rose smiled to herself at the preface in the McGuffey's Reader. It praised the book stating that words of only two or three letters were used at first. Then longer and more difficult ones would gradually be introduced. She looked forward to the day when the stories would be interesting and maybe, just maybe, captivate a young boy and introduce him to the world within books.

New words were presented at the start of each lesson and Tory learned them before going on to read the following pages. Rose followed up by having him copy the words on his slate. And it seemed to be working.

Rose taught using the Phonic Method. She had a phonic chart on a roller that she'd unwind, and together they'd sound out each letter as she pointed to it.

"Tory, you are getting faster than me in sounding out your letters," she praised at one lesson.

"Baby words," he scoffed, discarding her praise. "I'm still reading those stupid baby words like, 'The cat ran.' Who cares if the dog or cat ran or if the man had a pen? Or if a rat ran? I sure don't."

Rose laughed. She'd come to care deeply about this boy and saw that beneath his hard shell there was a highly intelligent young man. She didn't dare ask, but she sensed things might be better at home between him and Jesse.

Jesse continued to drop Tory off each morning and on the days she contrived to be standing on the top step at their arrival, all she got from the aloof man was a nod and a tip of his hat. Some days she imagined his eyes lingered on her back as she led the students inside. Once she turned to see, but all she got for her effort was a snap of the reins and the dust of the wagon as it pulled away from the school.

There was no reason for Jesse's handsome face to impose itself in her mind, coming forth at odd moments to tease her. No reason at all. And no reason at all for her heart to speed up on the rare occasions Tory might mention something Jesse did or said. And once when he shared what a terrible cook Jesse was, and how his effort at making a stew was so bad as to be un-edible, she joined Tory in laughter. Tory said even the chickens wouldn't eat it.

There were occasions when Rose found herself caught off guard and a warmth entered her, making her wish there were some way she could tell Jesse Rivers how much she admired him for trying so hard to be everything to Tory. Tory was the recipient of Jesse's patience and love. But who was there for Jesse?

Rose had to force herself to shake off that errant thought. Jesse Rivers wasn't her problem. And it certainly wasn't any of her business if the man received love or compassion. The very idea. Why, he didn't care one whit about her. He barely acknowledged her presence.

"Miss Bush." Tory's voice penetrated her musings.

"Sorry, Tory. My mind was elsewhere."

"Yeah, I had to yell at you."

Rose smiled. If he only knew where her mind had flown.

"What is it?" She placed another cookie on the plate in front of him. He'd already inhaled three but guessing the quality of the supper waiting him, another cookie could do little to spoil his appetite.

"I'm on lesson LIV."

"I know you are. You are about through the book. Can you tell me what numbers those Roman Numerals refer to?"

"Fifty-four," he said proudly.

"That's right."

"Well," he continued, "do you remember you told me about there being books on botany? You know, the names of the plants and flowers and all about them?"

"Yes, I remember."

Tory looked down at his empty plate. "I, uh, I was wondering . . ."

"Speak up, Tory. I can't hear you when you're talking to the dish."

He smiled up at her. Those rare smiles were coming more often.

"Do you think—"he started rambling, barely holding back his excitement—"do you think I could read outta that book yet?"

"I don't know. But there's one way to find out." Rose left the kitchen and went into the classroom returning with a thick book entitled, *Lessons and Manual of Botany.*

She placed the book in front of Tory.

Reverently, he traced the gold lettering on the hard cover. *"Lessons and Manual of Botany,"* Rose said.

Tory repeated the title, as again his fingers outlined each letter. Rose doubted that a man of faith approached the Bible with more reverence.

Rose turned the book so it was placed between them. "The words are difficult," she warned.

Tory nodded, his eyes never leaving the book.

"Well," she said with a smile in her voice, "it won't open itself. Tory, will you do the honors?"

"Huh?"

Rose chuckled. "Open the book, Tory. It won't bite you."

Gently, as though the pages would disintegrate at his touch, Tory opened to the Contents.

"Can you sound out any of the words here, or do any look familiar?"

"Mmmmorrr," he sounded, following his fingers over a word under the heading Section III.

"Mmmm," he tried again. Then he looked up at her, and Rose's heart melted at the look of defeat and anguish on his face.

"I can't," he mumbled.

"Sure you can. You just happened to pick an extremely difficult word. I'd have trouble sounding it."

"You would?" he said hopefully.

"Yes, I'm sure. The word is morphology. The pages under this section will be about the morphology of seedlings." Rose read from the book. *"Morphology is the branch of biology pertaining to the form and structure of plants."*

Tory's brow wrinkled and his eyes squinted with questions.

"Doesn't tell us much, does it?"

Disappointed, he shook his head.

"And that's why we have this book. To help us understand. Isn't it wonderful that a professional in this field took the time to write a book so that people like you and I could learn?"

"I-I guess so."

"Of course it is. So how would you feel about spending time after we finish our reading lesson studying this book?"

His eyes lit up. "You mean it? You think I could read it?"

"No, not yet, but I think it won't be long before you can. If you keep trying as hard as you are. Listen, Tory." She read another sentence. "*Red Maple seeds are ripe and ready to germinate at the beginning of summer.*"

"Red Maple." His tongue stroked the words. "We don't have Red Maples in Montana, do we?"

"No, but a botanist must learn about all plants and trees." Rose again scanned the preface of the book while talking. "This is interesting," she said excitedly then read the next sentence. "*Technical words may seem formidable but the study of botany will be the accumulation of knowledge and ideas.*"

"Formidable," he repeated. "Does that mean hard?"

"It does."

"Wow! Even the book knows the words are hard. It's not just me."

"No, it's not just you. You're not dumb, Tory. In fact, you're one of the brightest students in my class. You just got off to a slow start."

Nothing was said for a few minutes, both intent on the book in front of them.

Then, Tory jumped from his chair and threw his arms around her. "Thank you," he whispered.

Rose muffled a gasp.

Then, like a puff of smoke, Tory was out of the room, vanishing into the gathering dusk.

Rose got to her feet and, feeling light as a feather, moved about the kitchen. She'd won. She'd broken through the barrier. From now on, there would be no more battles to fight, no more hills to climb. Tory would continue to grow and learn.

She cut a slice of bread and realized that although she felt joy at reaching this special student, there was an empty space inside her still waiting to be filled. She hated to admit it, and fought the thought when it forced its way through, but the empty spot glowed on the rare occasions she allowed herself to think of Tory's brother—futile and foolish as that may be. But the time it really shone like a lantern in the dark of night was when she dreamed and planned for the future and the ranch she would someday have.

Chapter 17

A loud knock on the vestibule door jarred Rose out of her musings. Thinking Tory had returned, she hurried through the classroom and with a smile on her face she opened the door.

Seeing that instead of Tory, it was Mr. Whimpstutter, she felt her smile vanish like a thief in the night.

"Miss Bush." He gave a short nod and brushed past her.

"Uh." Rose swallowed the lump that magically appeared in her throat. "Mr. Whimpstutter. Do come in."

"What? Of course I'm in." He peered closely at her. "Are you all right, Miss Bush?"

"Yes, of course. I'm fine." She motioned toward her living quarters. "I was just having a cup of tea. Would you join me?"

"This is not a social call, Miss Bush. I am here as a representative of the school board. Regretfully, I am here to remind you that one of the rules governing teachers pertains to the, uh, entertaining a male in your private dwellings." He had the good grace to blush, but his pointed nose quivered like a skinny rat's, confronting a chunk of cheese.

"Entertaining?"

"Please do not interrupt, Miss Bush. We are quite aware that you have nightly assignations with a male student."

"A male student?" Parrot like, she repeated his words.

"Quite." He stretched his scarecrow frame. "Consistently you have dismissed your class except," and he paused squinting at her, "for one male student. You have been witnessed taking him into your kitchen and plying him with cookies."

"How?" What a stupid question. She knew how, but her mind wasn't connecting with her tongue.

"One of the students accidentally glanced in your kitchen window and was quite traumatized by what he saw."

"Accidentally?" Was she reduced to one-word questions?

"You are repeating my words, Miss Bush. This visit is difficult enough without your interruptions. Mrs. Chinney and Mrs. Backley were so shocked by such immoral actions, they begged off from confronting you. And while this is distasteful to me also, I must shield those two ladies and take on this onerous task myself."

Rose started to protest, to explain, only to be stopped by Mr. Whimpstutter's hand, palm out, in front of her face.

"As I was saying, this must not continue. Tonight concludes your meetings with this male student. Under no circumstances will you proceed with this . . . this distasteful and immoral conduct or your position as teacher in Wise River will be immediately terminated. Miss Bush, we have been very tolerant of your unorthodox methods of teaching. Even allowing pagan items to be hung in your classroom. And your refusal to use the rod is another issue. One that we will discuss at a later date when the ladies are present. To protect his own home-taught morals and Godly principles, a student has been forced to not participate in many of your lessons. This child thirsts for knowledge and is languishing."

"Willy." She loosened her tongue enough to spit out the name.

"I see you are aware of this."

"Mr. Whimpstutter. No, please allow me to explain." Rose ignored the hand again placed in front of her face. "The male is but a twelve-year-old boy that I am tutoring in reading."

"A dunce. A bully," Mr. Whimpstutter declared.

"A student. A student that is now able to read because of my tutoring."

"Oh, and I suppose the cookies played a part in this newfound ability?" he said snidely.

"No, but they put him at ease enough so he could relax and assimilate knowledge. I would do the same for any of my students. Tory Rivers was labeled and neglected by the former teacher. He is bright and anxious to learn."

"He is a male and you are violating the rules of conduct you agreed to," he thundered.

Rose shook her head in disgust and taking a deep breath tamped down the red mist of anger threatening to explode into the room.

"He is a child in need of special instruction. And I will continue to provide that instruction regardless of the small minds that construe this into something tawdry." She pursed her lips. "And regardless of a sneaky little boy that delights in causing trouble and peeking into my window. *For shame*."

Mr. Whimpstutter was shaking. His eyes bulged as he turned on his heel, and giving her one last glaring look, lost no time in exiting the room.

"You have been warned," he said ominously, and with head held high, he left, the door swinging in his wake.

Rose staggered from the room to her kitchen, grasping each passing desk to steady herself. Plopping down at the table, she realized the cozy room of a few short minutes ago had turned into a chilly emptiness. She wasn't wanted here. She didn't belong. This was not, and never could be, her home.

"What am I to do?" The sound of her voice hollow. "Teaching isn't my heart's desire, but I need this job." And feeling a magnitude of despair and helplessness, she took a sip of the cold tea and gazed at the nothingness.

"You're late," Jesse said to the boy blowing into the kitchen like a force of wind. "I almost ate this hunk of steak myself," Jesse teased, delighted that his and Tory's relationship had moved to where this was possible. Not only possible, but pleasurable. Jesse found himself thinking about and missing his brother during the day while he was at school. And oddly enough, as much as he resented it, he found himself envying Tory's time with the arrogant Teacher Bush.

"Teacher Bush kept you after school again, huh? Guess I'll go have a talk with her. You can't be that disruptive." Jesse wished he didn't have to play ignorant of the real reason Tory spent the extra time."

"Jesse," Tory said breathlessly, "I can read."

"What?" Jesse turned from the sink where he'd been scouring a skillet.

"I can read, Jesse. Here, let me show you." He dug around in the canvas bag and pulled out a small brown book.

Jesse fell into a chair opposite the young boy standing proudly at the head of the table.

"McGuffey's First Eclectic Reader. Revised Edition."

He raised his eyes, meeting Jesse's moist ones.

Puffing out his chest, Tory paged through to the back of the book. "These are the harder stories," he said proudly.

Jesse could only nod.

Tory held the book in front of his face, his brow wrinkled in concentration. *"We have come to the end of this book,"* he read. *"You can now read all the stories. You now need the second reader. Congrat—u—congratulations,"* he said loudly, looking expectantly at the man whose opinion mattered most.

Jesse moistened his lips and cleared his throat. Slowly, he shook his head.

"Darned if that isn't the best reading I've ever heard," he said in a choked voice. "It's like getting an early Christmas present hearing you spit out those hard words."

"Aww, it wasn't nothing," Tory fumbled.

"Nothing? I call it something. You are going to be a scholar, Tory. Maybe Teacher Bush does know her stuff."

"She does, Jesse, she does." Tory fell into a chair, waves of excitement shimmered from him. "I got to read out of the botany book. A real botany book. One with drawings and everything. Did you know red maple seed are ripe and"— he paused, his brow wrinkled as he searched his memory— "germinate, yeah they germinate in the spring?"

"No, I didn't know that. Red maple you say?" Jesse bit the inside of his cheeks to keep back his smile. This was serious business.

"Yep. 'Course we don't have red maple's here but Miss Bush says a botanist has to know about all plants and trees. Want to know something else?" he asked, suddenly acting shy.

"I sure do. This is terribly interesting. I'm hoping you'll share all your botany lessons with me. That way you could teach me as you learn."

"Huh?"

"Well, you're going to be a botanist so why not start with me?"

"You mean it?"

"I don't say things I don't mean, Tory."

"Okay. Here's something else I learned. I tried to sound out this word, but Miss Bush had to help me. I'm not dumb though," he said defensively, "just because I couldn't sound the word. See the book says those technical words are hard but that's what studying botany will teach me. The book"— he said the word like it was the Holy Bible, which to Tory it was— "The book knows the words are hard." He raised his chin, the words coming out mechanically, "Morphology is the shape of plants. Do you understand that, Jesse?"

"Well, I'm not sure I do. Could you explain?" It was all Jesse could do not to reach out and hug the budding botanist.

"Sure. It's the form a plant takes. How it looks. I have to know that so I can identify plants. I can draw them, but I have to recognize the form so I can put a name to them."

"Makes sense. You've picked something hard to learn, Tory. Lots harder than ranching."

"Naw."

But Jesse could see Tory was only trying to make him feel better. And he loved him for it.

Chapter 18

The weeks rolled by. Rose felt like she was sleepwalking through the days, waiting for the next perceived infraction that would bring about the school board's wrath. It was only a matter of time.

Recalling an incident that had happened last Friday, she her lips twitch in a very un-teacher like smile. And if there was a teensy bit of delight in her student's ingenuity, that wasn't wrong, was it?

Art and his group of cohorts, Timmy included, had locked Willy in the outhouse. The hot, smelly outhouse. They denied any knowledge of the deed, and by the time Rose had realized Willy hadn't returned from lunch recess, he'd been a guest of the wooden structure, with the tin roof that captured the sun's rays, for over an hour.

Rose questioned the class, asking if anyone knew Willy's whereabouts, but not one eye met hers. It was amazing how engrossed in slates and books they had all become. Willy was no one's favorite.

Rushing out the schoolhouse door, frantic in imagining all sorts of perils, she scanned the playgrounds. Alerted by knocks and a feeble voice coming from behind the wedged door, Rose rushed to his rescue. The red-faced boy that toppled out smelled to high-heavens. Not waiting for permission, he bolted for home. And every minute since then she'd felt like a convicted person must feel looking out the jailhouse window and seeing the gallows being built.

But today, she was looking forward to a visit from Wisteria and Robin. She would put her fears aside. It was

Saturday and they had decided to spend the day crocheting a rag rug. Wisteria had scoured the church's missionary barrel and had found several torn and unwearable dresses as well as some tattered men's shirts. They were unsuitable to send to missionaries, but perfect for what she and Rose had in mind.

"Come in," Rose called out to the knock on the kitchen door. "You don't need to knock, Wisteria."

The door opened, but it wasn't Wisteria that entered.

"Mr. Rivers." Rose hoped he didn't hear the breathless quality of her voice.

"Didn't mean to startle you."

"You didn't. I was just expecting someone else."

He raised his eyebrows.

"Wisteria. She and I are going to crochet a rug. She's gathering material now." Rose was aware she was rambling. Jesse Rivers wasn't interested in crocheting rugs. He must think her a dithering—what?—old-maid teacher?

"Would you like a cup of coffee?" Anxious to have something to do, Rose gripped the pot, turning toward the man.

"No, thanks. Been up since dawn. Musta drank a pot by now." Damn, but she was pretty. The flush on her cheeks made her skin look like porcelain.

Now it was his turn to be rattled. He'd had no intention to stop by the school when he'd come into town to pick up supplies. No intention at all. But it must have been in the back of his mind after all, because when he saw the white building with its bell steeple, he pulled the wagon to a quick stop. The fact that he'd been thinking about Rose Bush since Tory had come home excited that he could read certainly had nothing to do with it. He was just grateful to her for seeing in Tory what no one else had recognized. Shame flooded him. Not even he had looked that deep past the angry boy to see his love and thirst for knowledge. And botany would have never entered his mind. He owed Teacher Bush his thanks.

That was why he was here. To thank her. No other reason. It wasn't worth a second thought the fact that she looked especially pretty with the sun shining through the window, spinning her blonde curls to gold. He wasn't at all aware of her captivating eyes, blue as a summer sky, dominating her delicate face.

"Please have a seat, Mr. Rivers."

Rose's discomfort was obvious. Why was she so ill at ease? Was she concerned that Wisteria would be upset finding him in her kitchen? No, she was glancing behind him as though expecting an avenging angel to appear.

Uneasy, Jesse turned to see if someone had come in behind him. "Expecting someone besides your sister?" The fact that she might be looking so darned fetching for a suitor sent shards of jealousy through him. Shards as sharp as broken glass. Why should he care? Of course a single woman as beautiful as Rose Bush wouldn't stay unmarried for long in an area where women were a premium.

"No. No, just—"

"Just what?" He tried to keep the resentment out of his voice.

"It's just that the school board is watching me so closely."

"Why?"

Rose gave a sigh of resignation. "It doesn't matter, Mr. Rivers. That's my problem."

"Then why do I sense it's mine, too?"

"I'm sorry, but it's not you. It's me. You see, I violated one of the rules of conduct."

Jesse couldn't keep the grin from spreading across his face. "What'd you do, Teacher Bush, not ring the bell loud enough?"

"It's not a laughing matter, Mr. Rivers. I am inches away from being dismissed. And they'd like nothing more than to discover I'm entertaining another Rivers . . ." She clasped her hand to her mouth. "I-I didn't mean, I shouldn't have . . ."

"Sounds like you should have," he said harshly. "What did you mean by 'another Rivers?'"

"Nothing," Rose whispered. "Nothing at all."

"Oh, I think it is." He leaned back on his heels as his hand shot out and circled her arm. "Spill the beans, Teacher."

"Let go of me." She rubbed her arm when he quickly dropped it.

"Sorry. I didn't mean to grab you. Tell you what, let's both take a seat and you tell me why those righteous old biddies have it out for you."

"It's not just the two women, its Mr. Whimpstutter, too."

Jesse threw back his head and laughed, his teeth white in his tanned face. The sound filled the room, bringing with it a sense of comfort.

A fragile smile creased Rose's lips. Jesse Rivers would be a force to reckon with. With him in her kitchen, larger than life, she felt safe. For the first time since she'd left Wyoming, she felt as if she had someone to turn to for protection. That it was this man, a man who gave every impression of disliking her, was something to ponder later. But for now, he filled and dominated the room, owning it with his broad shoulders, the brown flecks in his penetrating eyes, and his air of supreme confidence. Reluctantly, she took a chair opposite him as a sense of calm and ease entered her.

"Whimpstutter," Jesse said, "lives up to his name. He's a wimp, a bully that uses his position to strut about town like he's damned important. Men like him don't deserve . . ." His words dwindled off as understanding broke through. "Tory. It's you tutoring Tory that's the problem, isn't it?"

Rose slowly nodded. "Yes." She dragged out the word. "As Mr. Whimpstutter phrased it, I'm guilty of entertaining a man in my kitchen, plying him with cookies." She raised her long eyelashes and a cute dimple appeared at the side of her full mouth. "Plying him with cookies. A young boy." She spit out the words, her indignation and disgust evident.

"Did you explain what you were doing, that you were teaching him to read?"

"Yes, how did you know?"

"Overheard you two in the woods when you made him bargain to stay all day at school and you wouldn't tell me about his leaving." His lips quirked as he saw the dismay cross her face.

"I kept it from you," she said softly.

"You sure did."

"I had to. I had to have something to hold over Tory. Something that would make him remain in the classroom. Something that would make him apply himself to reading." Rose looked up at him, her eyes shining. "He's smart, Jesse. He's so smart."

"I know."

"You know?"

"I just didn't know how smart until you took the time to bring it out of him."

Rose looked away, embarrassed, yet so very pleased at his praise.

Jesse got to his feet. "I came by to thank you. And now that I know it's put your job in jeopardy, I feel I owe you more than thanks. I'll take care of Whimpstutter."

"No!" Rose exploded from her chair. "Please. While teaching isn't my heart's desire, I need this job. I need to save as much money as I can. I have to, Mr. Rivers." She was back to the formality. "I have to."

"Why?" Jesse demanded an explanation. And Rose knew he wouldn't leave until he got it.

"Because," she said, not looking at him, "because it's the only way I'll get back my dream."

Jesse didn't move, but he never took his eyes off her.

"What dream, Teacher Bush?" he gently asked.

"My dream of having my own ranch. I had it once, but lost it. This time, this time I'll be smarter. This time I'll fight harder and never, never give up." She raised her head. "I'm a rancher, Mr. Rivers. It's in my blood and I'll never be happy doing anything else."

With a grave expression on his face, Jesse said, "I wish you luck. I know exactly how you feel. I won't interfere, but I'll be there waiting, should you ever need me."

And with that he was gone, taking with him her sense of security, as well as the sunshine from the room.

Chapter 19

"Oh, Wisteria." Rose moved aside the rug they were crocheting. "You should have seen him. No, smelled him. Oh my gosh." Tears streamed down their faces as they shamelessly giggled over the outhouse incident. "He was beet red and hoarse. I stepped back but still the smell . . ."

"Stop. Rose, stop." Wisteria clutched her stomach. "I can just smell him, the weasely little brat." She sank weakly into the kitchen chair, shoulders shaking with each giggle.

"I can laugh with you now, but I won't be laughing when Mrs. Backley sweeps into my classroom like a prairie twister." She recounted Mr. Whimpstutter's visit and warning earlier to Wisteria.

"This will be icing on the cake, I'm afraid."

Wisteria wiped her eyes and became serious. "I know, hon, I know. I feel so bad for coaxing you here and into this predicament. But I wanted you close, and it seemed like the right thing."

"It was." Rose patted her hand and pushed the cup of hot tea closer. "How could you know that Wise River Montana was home to such a narrow-minded trio?"

"If I hadn't been so wrapped up in myself and our new life here, I would have been more aware."

"Yes"—Rose took a bite of cookie—"and I suppose if you hadn't driven by the Colorado River that day and found Dr. Ben McCabe half in the water, burning up with fever, none of this would have transpired."

"It wouldn't have. But then" —smiles wreathed her

face—"I wouldn't have drug him into my wagon, and sweet Robin and I wouldn't have him to love."

Wisteria's eyes darkened with the memory of finding Ben, a convict just recently released from Yuma Territorial Prison where he'd spent four years for a crime he didn't commit. Four years of torture and depravation. Four years that had left him half-dead, unfeelingly deposited there by a wagon driver paid to take him to the nearest town. Left burning-up with fever and raw, oozing sores from too tight shackles. If she hadn't been returning from an infrequent trip to town with baby Robin asleep on the wagon seat, Ben would have laid there, unseen and forgotten. It was nothing short of a miracle, she'd seen him. Tara, her mare, had shied, seeing the body, and the rest was history.

Lee, her brother-turned-outlaw and Robin's father, had died in a gun battle. She'd been given Robin to love as well as Ben. Theirs hadn't been an easy love. But when it came out that Ben had been trained to be a doctor, first under his sister-in-law, Aries, and then the prison doctor, he'd been convinced to return to Wise River, Montana and his family who had thought him dead. They had married. Robin loved her 'En and it was certainly reciprocated. She was his shadow.

"Wipe that cat-licking-cream look off your face and tell me what you're thinking," Rose said, breaking through Wisteria's musings.

"About Ben and how he came into my life. I love him so much, Rose. But I'm also worried about him."

"Why?" Rose frowned. "He's not sick is he?"

"No," Wisteria chuckled. "He's almost too well. He's pushing himself too hard, taking on more and more of Aries' patients."

"She's close to having that baby, isn't she?"

"Yes, and I don't know who's the most excited. Little sister-to-be, Angelique, Daddy Jarrett, Grandpa Ted, Uncle

Timmy, or Momma? They're quite a family out there on the Big Hole Valley Ranch."

"Yes, they are. I've only been out to their ranch once, but it's beautiful."

"Located close to the Rocking R and that good-looking Jesse Rivers, too."

"Wisteria," Rose said in pretended horror. "You're a married woman."

"Happily married." Wisteria laughed. "But I'm not blind, and you'd have to be blind not to notice Jesse Rivers, that defiant chin and angry eyes."

"He's rude and arrogant."

"And strong."

"Very," Rose agreed, remembering how safe he made her feel. "But he's like a big cat, a predator."

Wisteria chuckled. "Rose, you've been reading those books again, haven't you?"

"No. I'm just telling you what he reminds me of."

"Mmm-hmm. And your eyes are telling me something else."

"What are you going to do about Ben?" Rose asked, changing the subject. "He'll have even more to handle when Aries has the baby and takes the time off she promised Jarrett.

"You can change the subject, Rose, but Jesse Rivers makes a secret smile appear on your face. That's all I'm going to say."

"Thank heavens."

"But about Ben. I don't know what to do other than make his home a haven to return to. He loves being a doctor."

"The people love him. You know, Wisteria, I envy him."

"You do?" Wisteria asked.

"Yes. He's following his life's dream. I'm not. I'm teaching children who deserve someone that delights in teaching young minds. I'm not saying I don't enjoy them. But . . ."

"But it's not ranching," Wisteria interrupted. "It's not getting up before the sky is light and working until its dark.

It's not shoveling manure, pulling bloody, slimy, calves from their mother's body in the freezing cold. It's not lifting back-breaking pitchforks full of hay in a Wyoming blizzard. Yes, sister dear, I can easily see how you must miss it."

"Scoff." Rose chuckled. "I'll have it back someday. And this time I'll make it work."

"I know you will." Wisteria kept her voice soft.

Of the three sisters, Rose was the strongest and the most determined. Her petite frame often fooled people, but she was someone, as the settlers would say, to cross the river with. It wasn't fair what she had to endure at the school board's hands. Jealous, small-minded people bent on doing her sister harm. Tonight, she'd talk to Ben. He always had the answers.

"That rug isn't getting made while we sit here eating cookies and drinking tea," Rose said.

"No, but next to your chocolate cake, I like your molasses cookies best."

"That's not what you said your last visit. You said it was my bread. Or was it my bread pudding? No that was before that."

"Laugh, Miss Bush, but there's no denying you can cook."

Rose nudged the cookie plate closer to Wisteria. "I love being here with you, sister mine. And no matter what the outcome, I don't regret for one minute coming. Bring on the school board. They don't scare me. Well, not much."

Chapter 20

It had been two weeks since Mr. Whimpstutter's visit and Rose was beginning to breathe easier. There were even times she was able to forget, and the work with Tory went on as before. A stubborn streak in her took impish delight in disregarding Mr. Whimpstutter's dire warnings. But in an effort to be somewhat compliant, she invited Timmy McCabe to stay after class, too. Rose made sure the kitchen curtains were pulled back so that should anyone 'happen' to look in, they would see an innocent setting—two boys doing schoolwork. Of course, cookies were offered, but books were open and both boys studiously bent over them. Tory was entranced in the botany book and Timmy was interested in anything medical. Not as one might think, medicine related to humans. No, his interest lay in doctoring animals. Thankfully, his sister Aries, being a physician, recognized this and saw that he was supplied with veterinary books. Several of which he brought with him. Rose wondered if it was the lure of her cookies or his growing friendship with Tory that made him agreeable to staying after school. Whatever it was, she was grateful for his presence.

After Jesse's visit to thank her for tutoring Tory, he once again pulled back into his shell and avoided any contact with Rose, other than the mannerly tip of his fingers to the brim of his hat and a curt nod. Rose realized his smiles were rare where she was concerned, but plentiful when directed toward Tory. And if she resented that fact, she hid it well.

Thanksgiving had sneaked by, and the classroom changed from a peaceful fall atmosphere to one of heightened intensity as Christmas got closer each day. Now the talk was of presents and the much-looked-forward-to prospect of school being out for two wonderful weeks.

Rose decided that in addition to having the expected Christmas performance, the students would pick different countries and learn about their customs. They would work together in small groups and share their findings with the assembled parents and townspeople. This would be interspersed with selected Christmas songs. It would be a much different program from the expected recitations, biblical, and otherwise.

When she presented this to the class, it was greeted with enthusiasm and delight in doing something different. It turned out that the majority of the class wanted to be a part of the group learning how the Chinese celebrated Christmas. With great eagerness they decided to follow the custom and make a fake dragon. Candles would be decorated in the Chinese tradition of red and gold. Rose delighted in hearing them try to wrap their tongue around the Chinese word for Merry Christmas, or correctly, Holy-birth happy.

The remainder of the class chose to talk about how the early Dutch settlers celebrated Christmas or St Nicholas Eve. The poem "A Visit From St. Nicholas" was to be memorized and given. And not to be outdone by the Chinese group, they would learn the Dutch word for St. Nicholas.

The night of the Christmas Chorale performance was crisp and clear. Rose watched from the sidelines as each child showed their parents around the classroom and encouraged them to sit in their desks. Smiles were on every face except that of Jesse Rivers. He wasn't smiling, but he was there, his large hand resting on Tory's shoulder as the boy showed off his drawings and his unique desk.

When the time came for the performance to begin, parents took their seats on the chairs from Rose's kitchen and the McCabe's home. Excitement hung in the air along with the enticing smell of the molasses cookies set out on a table in the back of the room. Two of the older girls stood proudly by the cookies, having baked them in Rose's kitchen. The boys, their faces scrubbed and hair slicked down, proudly took arms and escorted parents to their seats. Rose, a smile on her lips, nodded approval to each child, as proud as a mother hen showing off her flock of chicks. The evening was in the students' hands. They had planned it, and other than her presence, nothing was required of her.

Mrs. Backley sat in a chair close to Willy's desk. Her back ramrod straight and she wore a peacock-proud look on her face. Willy, unlike the homespun look of the other children, wore a suit, resplendent with a string tie. That he was sadly out of place did not enter either smug mind.

Mrs. Chinney and Mr. Whimpstutter sat on either side of Mrs. Backley, heads up and noses tilted and pointed. An aura of gravity and somber authority enveloped them.

Rose swallowed hard as she met their censorious looks and sent up a fervent prayer that the evening would be a success.

The first song, "Silent Night," was perfect. Even Willy, marching to the front of the room to give a sonorous reading from the bible about the Christ child's birth, was well received. Especially by the three judges, as Rose thought of them. It seemed the mood had been set, and she gave a sigh of relief. That it was premature was soon to be discovered.

Another Christmas song was sung, then the Dutch group went to the front of the room and told about the Dutch's patron saint, St. Nicholas. Dutch children hung stockings on St. Nicholas Eve in early December, hoping they would be filled with presents. Two of the girls recited the poem "A Visit From St. Nicholas" and told how it was first published anonymously in a newspaper in Troy, New York, December 23, 1823.

"And," they finished, "we now know it was written by Clement Clarke Moore." Then in a loud voice, the group called out *"Sinterklaas,"* the Dutch word for St. Nicholas.

Parents applauded and beamed. All except the formidable three. If at all possible, their backs were stiffer, heads higher, noses more tilted, and the aura surrounding them grimmer. Three sets of eyes glared at Rose. St. Nicholas, indeed.

Frantically, she motioned for the singing to start, hoping the music would work a calming effect.

Several well-known Christmas songs were sung with parents joining in.

Then Rose announced there would be a short break while the last group prepared for their presentation. She motioned to the table of cookies and punch in the back of the room and the beaming girls ready to serve them.

When the last cookies were eaten and the punch bowl was empty, the smiling parents sat back down. During the intermission, Rose had received many words of praise and thanks. Enough that she was able to ignore the fact that she was not acknowledged or approached by the three members of the school board or by Jesse Rivers.

Then when all was quiet, the Chinese group took their places in the front of the room for the final presentation. One-by-one they told about Chinese customs and how Christmas was celebrated in China. Rose cast an anxious glance around the room. A look of interest was on most faces. Perhaps she was worrying for nothing. The night was going well, wasn't it?

Cloth-decorated red-and-gold candles came out and were pantomimed being hung out of windows. Then a voice rang out saying that street parties with "fake dragons" were held. With those two words, the connecting door to Rose's quarters burst open and with a great roar, out pranced a gaudy dragon. Its paper head and decorated sheet body was draped over several students who immediately began a sinuous winding around the room, stopping every so often to roar. This was accompanied by shouts of *"Shengdan Kuaile"* pronounced shnng-dan kwy-ler or Holy-birth happy. Laughter and fake cries of fear greeted the dragon as parents and children alike took part in the dragon's tour of the room. It wound its way back to rest by the remainder of the group waiting importantly in the front of the room. Then the narrator spoke the final words. "Most of the Chinese people are not Christian."

A gasp surged from the school board's outraged lips. Shaking the rafters of the building, it fell into the hushed room. Rising to their feet as one, Mrs. Backley jerked Willy out of his seat, and with vindicated wrath, they flounced toward the door, loudly uttering, *"Blaspheme, pagan, unchristian, unacceptable."* Mrs. Backley paused at the door, her hands held protectively over Willy's ears. He wore a satisfied smile on his lips.

"We have tried to be open-minded of your unusual methods of teaching, Miss Bush," she said in a deafening voice, "but this blasphemous corruption of young minds will not be tolerated. You have gone too far. I can assure you, you will be hearing from us."

The door slammed behind them, and Rose knew it was slamming shut not only on the schoolroom, but also on her short-lived career as teacher.

Silently, she watched as parents filed from the room. There were many hasty looks of commiseration, but Rose didn't stay to see them. Head held high, and with as much pride as possible, she slowly walked into her private quarters and firmly shut the door behind her.

Chapter 21

"Rose, open the door. I know you're in there. Listen, sister mine, I'll stand here all day, but I *will* talk to you. I didn't force you to open up yesterday, but I'm not letting you shut yourself inside that schoolhouse any longer."

Quiet greeted Wisteria's words, then slowly, inch by inch, the door opened. Wisteria swept through the narrow opening, marching past a silent Rose and the empty rows of desks. She stepped inside Rose's private quarters and took a deep breath as the stark coldness hit her. It was dark, curtains pulled, and void of life. An overwhelming sense of emptiness hung in the air. There was no welcoming glow from the kitchen range, no merrily hissing teakettle. There was a sense of abandonment, as though no one lived here anymore. She looked past her sister at the large trunk resting at the foot of the bed.

"Going somewhere?"

"Yes," Rose said softly, "but I'm not sure where."

Wisteria felt a flush of anger. "They fired you, didn't they?"

"No."

"No?"

"No. I didn't give them the satisfaction." Rose's eyes sparked fire. "I quit. I gave my notice yesterday. They have time before school starts back in January to find a replacement."

"Good for you. I hope you gave them a piece of your mind."

Rose grinned. "I think it's safe to say I left them speechless."

"Grab your bonnet, sis, let's get out of here. And don't tell me you don't know where you're going. I'm taking you home to my house. We'll have Ben pick up your trunk." She glanced around the room. "Looks like you're all packed."

"I am. But, Wisteria, I can't impose on you and Ben."

"You're not imposing, Rose. We're family."

"And I love you for offering, but I told Mr. Whimpstutter I would remain here until the end of December. By then I hope to have found work somewhere. Work and a place to live," she added with determination.

"Rose, I can't let you stay here." Wisteria swept her hand across the room. "It's like a tomb. All the life is gone."

"Because I let the fire go out. When I get it going again, some of the chill will leave. Don't worry about me. You know I always land on my feet."

"I know you're also very stubborn." Wisteria gave an exasperated sigh. "Please, Rose. Stay with us at least until you find something."

Rose's bark of laughter filled the room. "Be careful, little sister. That could take some time. But there will be something," she said, the words forceful. "Something until I get my . . ." Rose swallowed.

"Until you get your ranch." Wisteria's voice rose in exasperation. "Are you ever going to give up that dream? Don't you realize ranching isn't possible for a woman alone? I'll say it again, stop being stubborn."

"I'm not being stubborn—"

A man's voice cut off her sentence. "Sounds like stubbornness to me."

Rose whirled around. Jesse Rivers' wide shoulders filled the doorway. A scowl marred his handsome face. His narrowed gaze bored into hers and the silence grew. He gave a short nod at Wisteria, then tilted his chin toward the trunk. "That everything? I haven't got all day."

"I-I beg your pardon?" Rose backed up one step and crossed her arms defensively. "This is none of your business, Mr. Rivers."

He gave a half shrug. "I'm making it my business." His eyes were dark and fathomless as he met and held her gaze. They never left her face as he said in that same hard as flint voice, "Sorry, Mrs. McCabe, "but I'll be taking Miss Bush to my ranch."

Before Wisteria could utter one word, Rose flew across the room until she was toe to toe with the formidable man. "You'll be taking me to your ranch?" she repeated, venom dripping of each word. "I don't think so. Just who put you in charge of my life?"

"Somebody has to be in charge. You don't seem to be."

Rose lips narrowed into a fine line and the words hissed from her mouth. "Listen, Mr. High and Mighty Rivers, I've had a rough few days. Much more of your superior attitude, and I'll forget I'm a lady. Now get out."

"Rose," Wisteria cautioned in a whisper.

Jesse had to bite back a smile. The little lady in front of him was a fighter, no doubt about it. Admiration filled him. Admiration and something else he refused to recognize.

He moved past Rose as if she wasn't there and, bending over, hefted the trunk to his shoulder. "What'd you pack in here, part of the stove?" he grunted, moving with ease out the door.

"Mr. Rivers, you stop. You stop right now. Put that trunk down or I'll . . ."

Calmly, ignoring the woman dogging him, Jesse reached the wagon and slid the trunk into the back. Then he turned, facing the fire-breathing Rose and an anxious Wisteria.

"I don't have time to sugar-coat this, Miss Bush. Like I said inside, you're coming to my ranch."

Rose glared at him, hands on her hips. "And like I said inside, what I do or don't do is none of your business.

I'm . . . I'm going home with," she gulped, "with Wisteria. Get my trunk out of your wagon. Now!"

Jesse looked past her at an ashen Wisteria, her mouth forming a startled O.

"I apologize, Mrs. McCabe. I have a horse ready to foal and chores waiting to be done. I tend to be a bit abrupt when I'm trying to do two things at once."

"Hmmpf," Rose snorted. "Abrupt, pushy, arrogant, obstinate, and hard of hearing."

"I'm offering your sister a job," Jesse said as if Rose hadn't spoke at all.

"A job? You're offering me a job?"

Jesse riveted his eyes on her. "Yes, I'm offering you a job. Why else would I want you on my ranch?"

"Why else indeed," Rose snapped.

"Now get down off'n your high-horse and get in the wagon. Like I said, I don't have all day."

"Mr. Rivers. I'll speak slowly so you'll understand, I am not your problem. You do not need to invent a 'job' for poor pitiful me."

Anger flashed in his eyes and he spoke through clenched teeth. "Damn it, Rose Bush, you make it hard to feel anything but an urge to turn you over my knee and teach you some manners."

Wisteria giggled, drawing a withering look from Rose.

"No one would pity you," Jesse said. "They'd pity the poor fool that had to put up with you." He held up his hand, stopping the words threatening to jump from her mouth. "I need a housekeeper. Tory's a growing boy and needs someone that can cook. Hell, I need someone that can cook. I've tasted your cake and that alone qualifies you for the job. I can't spend my time caring for a house, cooking, and doing all the chores I plan to pile on you. It's a job. A paying job." He quoted a figure that made Rose's eyes pop.

"You'll pay me that much?" she asked, obviously in awe.

"You'll earn every penny of it. In fact, after a few weeks, you'll probably think I'm not paying enough."

"Does that include room and board?"

"Yes." For the first time Jesse allowed his lips to curl into a short smile. "Money talks, huh, Miss Bush?"

"It does," she snapped. "How long do you plan to hire me as your housekeeper?"

"As long as you'll stay, providing, that is, you can keep that fiery temper in check and your impudent mouth closed."

"Can you?"

"Huh?"

"I said, 'Can you?' Can you keep your temper in check and your know-it-all attitude under control?"

"I don't have a temper, and my attitude isn't up for discussion." He threw the words back at her. "But you could make a preacher cuss."

Rose chose to ignore his protest. "I won't promise beyond a year, maybe less. It all depends on how much money I can . . ."

"I know," he said patronizingly, "how much you can save to buy another homestead. I couldn't help overhearing, and I know you lost your last one. No reason you can't save every penny I pay you. Unless"—an impish twinkle entered those hazel eyes—"you buy more of those ridiculous hats."

"And that is something else that is none of your business, Mr. Rivers." Rose took a deep breath. "Where will I live?"

"In the house with Tory and me. There's four bedrooms, two unoccupied. You can have your pick. Sorry, I don't have someplace else that would be adequate."

"Fine." Rose moved toward the wagon seat.

"Rose," Wisteria put a hand on her sister's arm. "Rose, what are you thinking? You can't move in with a single man and a young boy. What will people think?"

"Wisteria, love, you know by now I don't give a tinker's damn what people think."

Chapter 22

They were turning onto the lane leading to the Rocking R before Rose broke the silence.

"Mr. Rivers."

"Miss Bush?"

"I would like to get settled in before we discuss what you consider my duties are, and what I agree they are."

Jesse grinned. "You forgetting already that I'm the boss? Your 'duties' are what I ask you to do, nothing less."

"Oh, I don't think so. I'm your housekeeper, not your slave."

"Yep, you're my housekeeper all right. Although at this minute I'm wondering why I thought I needed one."

Rose bristled. "Then my advice is to stop wondering and turn this wagon around."

Jesse pulled the reins to a stop in front of the large ranch house. "Nope."

"Nope?"

He turned to Rose. "Like I said, I need a housekeeper. Tory needs someone to provide him with decent meals. And," he added as if an afterthought, "I hope you'll continue to tutor him. I regret that's part of what got you into this mess, but I don't regret your taking the time and putting your teaching position at risk to help him."

"So that's it."

Jesse frowned. "What's it?"

"That's the reason why you all of a sudden decided you needed a housekeeper. You're offering me this trumped up job because you feel guilty. I'll have you know I don't need your charity." Rose jumped down from the wagon seat, fluffed out her skirt, and setting her hat firmly on her head, proceeded to march back up the lane.

"Just a minute," Jesse barked as he vaulted from the wagon and grabbed her arm. "Where do you think you're going?"

"Since you seem inclined to not turn the wagon back to town, I'm walking there. I'll send someone for my trunk." She tried to jerk away from his vise-like grip. "Let go of my arm, Mr. Rivers. This is the second time you've grabbed me. I won't put up with being manhandled."

Jesse dropped her arm as if it were a red-hot poker. "Sorry," he said, shamefaced. "I-I wouldn't hurt you, uh, manhandle you, or anyone, for that matter." He shook his head and muttered, "Damn my temper."

Perplexed, Rose furrowed her brow at his fervent apology.

"I'm sure you wouldn't hurt me, Mr. Rivers. I know you wouldn't." She felt compelled to reassure the contrite man. Why was he overreacting? "Perhaps I spoke too quickly. Sometimes"—she smiled—"I, too, have a temper. That's something we have in common. That, and the fact we seem to rub each other the wrong way. What about us calling a truce, going inside and discussing this 'job' calmly over, say, a cup of coffee? I don't know about you, but so far, today has been a reason to crawl back in bed and pull the covers over your head."

"That about sums it up." He looked worriedly at her arm. "Are you sure you're okay?"

"Absolutely. Now if you'll direct me to your kitchen, I'll perform my first duty as a housekeeper and make a pot of coffee. Have you had your noon meal yet?" Rose asked, fingering the chain holding her precious timepiece. She popped open the small cover. "Goodness, it's two o'clock. Of course you have," she said, answering her own question.

Jesse breathed a sigh of relief at Rose's change of heart and shook his head. "Afraid not. Tory and I had a breakfast of sorts. He cooked," Jesse added. "We, uh, we usually skip the noon meal and make it until dinner. Two meals a day of our cooking is about all we can handle." He gave a shamefaced grin, deepening the dimple in his cheek.

Rose gulped. The man was too good looking for his own good, or hers either, as a matter of fact. Well, she wasn't here to be lured in by Jesse Rivers' handsome face. No. She had a job to do and money to save.

"That will stop as of today. Please carry my trunk to my room. Whichever one you choose is fine with me. And I'll look over your kitchen. I'm assuming you have foodstuff necessary to make a meal? Where's Tory? Let him know we will be having an early supper. Tomorrow we'll have breakfast, and our main meal will be at noon, unless you're unable to come to the house . . . and the reason had better be good," she said under her breath. "Supper will be light. We'll work out the times later. I'll see you back in the kitchen for coffee. We can discuss my duties while I prepare an early supper. I can assure you, Mr. Rivers, it will be substantial. Tory will not be missing any more meals, nor will he be doing any more of the cooking."

Jesse blinked twice, momentarily at a loss for words, or how to respond to Rose's about-face and rapidly fired words, other than to open the door to the kitchen and wave her inside. The woman should have been a general in the army. She had a gift for giving orders and fully expecting them to be obeyed. And, surprisingly, there was no question he'd do just that. Oddly enough, there wasn't an ounce of resentment or reluctance in him. He gave a sigh of relief as he went outside to the wagon. Rose Bush had arrived, and darned if it didn't feel right.

Rose plunked the thick, white mug in front of Jesse and gave him a reproachful look. "You should be ashamed of yourself, Jesse Rivers. Your shelves are stocked better than the mercantile. I haven't had time to look at your smokehouse or cellar, but I'd wager a guess they're not meager."

"I don't deny that there's plenty here to cook, Miss Bush, but you have to know how to prepare it. Just the same, Tory and I haven't starved," he said defensively, taking a sip of the perfectly brewed coffee. "Still, if you need something I don't have, make a list and I'll pick it up when I go to town, or better yet, you can take the wagon to town yourself. You do know how to drive a wagon, don't you?"

Rose took the seat across from Jesse and eyed him through the steam rising from her mug. "I think you need to know something about me, Mr. Rivers."

Jesse opened his mouth to object only to be quelled by the look on Rose's face.

"I'm not a schoolmarm no matter that you call me Teacher Bush. I never pretended to be a teacher and did not hesitate to make it clear that the position was to be an end to a means." She absently brushed back a golden strand of hair that had managed to escape from the knot at the nape of her neck. It curled winsomely around her face, coaxing out the blue in her eyes.

"I am a rancher. Pure and simple. I can handle any job thrown at me and do it as well as most men. I'm not bragging, simply stating a fact. I worked hard on my homestead and would have made it if the fever hadn't wiped out my herd. I pride myself on my baking, but I'm also equally proud of my being able to ride, rope a steer, fix fence, calf, brand, and the myriad of other chores associated with ranching."

So intent on her speech, Rose missed the twinkle that had appeared in Jesse's eyes.

"And"—she took a deep breath—"I can milk a cow, feed chickens, plant a garden, and put up the bounty. I—"

"A cow? You had a milk cow on a ranch?"

"Of course I did. I had pigs and chickens, too. Ranching isn't exclusive to beef and horses, Mr. Rivers. I provided for myself any way I could. But what you don't know is how much I loved it. All of it, even the long hours and the back-breaking work."

"Seems like I'm always apologizing to you, Miss Bush. I've underestimated you." He smiled. "You look delicate, but to think that would be a grave misunderstanding. I'm sure I'm not the first person to make that mistake. You look like you belong in a rich man's house with servants to do your bidding."

"I'd hate it," she said forcefully. Then she smiled back at him as she took another sip of coffee. "I'll take that as a compliment, though. But please don't assume I can't do anything pertaining to ranching. I know Wisteria thinks I'm crazy, but I plan on having my own place again. This time I'll be more prepared."

"I don't mean to disagree with you, but ranching is filled with surprises. You can't be prepared for everything." Jesse got to his feet, surprised at how easy it had been to forget his waiting chores and visit with this captivating woman over a cup of coffee. He'd have to be careful or it would become a habit.

"I'll see you later at supper." He put his hat on his head, grabbed his coat and headed out the door. "I'm running behind so I guess that talk'll wait."

"Give me a couple hours, Mr. Rivers," Rose called after him.

"Ring the bell on the porch. That's how Emma called us in."

Chapter 23

Jesse looked across the table at Tory and winked, pushing back his chair. "I don't believe I could eat another bite. That was the best meal I've had in too long to remember."

"Yeah," Tory chimed in, "me, too. I wasn't sure I'd like it when I saw the steak wasn't burned. I've gotten real used to that black crunch with every bite."

Jesse reached over and playfully cuffed the boy's head. "I'm sure Miss Bush would set aside your steak from now on and cook it just the way you like it."

"Sit back down, Mr. Rivers. Unless"—Rose paused, a teasing look on her face—"you don't like, or have room for, dried apple cobbler."

Jesse made a show of falling back into his chair and groaning. "I knew it. I've died and gone to heaven. Cobbler, you said?"

"Mmm, hmm, dried apple. Now if we had our own milk cow, I'd be able to put cream on the top. Thick, rich cream. And I'd make sweet butter, cold, refreshing buttermilk, and hard cheese, although I have to admit I never did get the cheese-making down pat."

"Cream?" Tory asked. "When I go over to the Watson's for eggs, Billy always brags about having berries and cream or cream on his oatmeal instead of milk." He looked over at Jesse. "I hate havin' to buy anything from him. He's a loud-mouthed bully."

"Tory," Rose admonished. "You're displaying a poor attitude. Don't you know bullies have one reason for being the way they are?"

"What's that?" he asked suspiciously.

"They're jealous."

"Jealous," he scoffed. "Of me?"

"Of course, of you. Why not you?"

Jesse's eyes darted between the two of them. If Rose Bush could build up Tory's poor self-esteem, he'd buy her that darn cow, and throw in a few chickens besides.

"You're smart, talented, you have your own horse, and you're part owner in a ranch that is probably larger than Billy's. Am I right?"

"Well," he said reluctantly, "you've got the horse and ranch part right." His chest expanded and his eyes held an unmistakable light. "My horse is a pinto, and I am partners in a bigger spread."

"And . . .?" Rose prodded.

"And, that's all, I guess."

"You guess?" She gave Tory her firm teacher's look. "You guess? You know darned good and well you're smart, Tory Rivers. And talented," she added. "You have a gift. You're not only on your way to being a botanist, something Billy Watson knows nothing about, but you're an artist. In a few years your talent will be recognized by one of the universities. They'll pay for your education, mark my words."

"You really think so, Miss Bush?" Tory's voice squeaked. "A university?"

Rose nodded emphatically.

Jesse couldn't take his eyes off her. This bossy, determined woman was peeling back the layers of self-doubt and unworthiness beaten into his brother. And she was doing it effortlessly, with honesty and conviction.

Rose picked up the cobbler and started to dish large spoonfuls into waiting bowls. "Now, the next time you go to the Watson's for eggs, you hold your head up high. Nothing Billy says will get under your skin. Understand me?" She pinned Tory with a fierce look. "Because if you don't, you'll answer to me."

Tory smiled and said the words Rose swore she'd never have to hear again.

"Yes, Miss Bush."

"Hmmpf," she muttered, placing the bowls in front of the two who were eyeing them with delight and anticipation. "As soon as you're finished, you need to get right on the chores Jesse has set out for you. Because"—She paused.—"after he and I finish discussing my"—she cleared her throat and gave Jesse a hard look—"duties, we'll start on your lessons."

"My lessons," Tory protested. "It's Christmas break. Why do I have to have lessons when no one else does? All the other kids are free."

"Yes, and all the other kids aren't preparing to enter a university. There will be lessons every night, Tory Rivers." Rose's hands were resting on her shapely hips.

Jesse had to look away. More of her hair had escaped the tight bun while she'd been cooking supper. Her face was flushed to a rosy glow, and darned if it didn't seem as if she'd been a part of this big kitchen forever. It was a quelling thought to realize Rose Bush looked as though she belonged in this empty, memory-filled house. And along with that realization was the fact that laughter and happiness had crept in alongside this woman who wasn't afraid to fight for what she wanted and believed in. If she thought Tory was university material, then he was. It was as simple as that. Jesse wasn't aware that a piece of ice had broken away from his heart.

"Yes, Ma'am," Tory mumbled, his spoon halfway to his mouth.

"I thought so." Rose dished up a smaller bowl of cobbler for herself and took her chair across from Jesse.

"How is it, Mr. Rivers?"

"If it was any better, I'd be whimpering, Miss Bush. I thought your chocolate cake heavenly, but I do believe this cobbler is right up there with it."

"Did Tory get his piece of that chocolate cake or did you eat it all yourself?"

"Nope, darndest thing, I put that cake right there on that counter and when I came down the next morning, it was gone. Just a few crumbs left. Now I know for a fact Tory didn't eat it. He'd made it plain he didn't want any."

Tory hunched over his bowl as he focused entirely on the last bit of cobbler.

Rose caught Jesse's eye and winked. His stomach clenched and he knew he'd better get out of that kitchen before he did or said something foolish.

"Come on, Tory," he growled, reverting back to his safe abrupt manner. "If you scrape that bowl any harder the flowers will come off into your spoon. We've got chores to do."

With a surprised look on his face, Tory jumped from his chair and followed Jesse out through the mudroom door.

"Supper was good, Miss Bush. Thank you." With those terse words, Jesse firmly shut the door behind him and the beautiful woman gracing his table.

"Jesse Rivers, you are a rude, irascible man," Rose muttered to the empty room. "Well, I don't have to like you to work for you. And I don't like you," she lied to herself. "Not one little bit."

She poured hot water out of the teakettle into the dishpan and began washing the dishes. Her anger fueled her, and in short time the task was completed. Then, curiosity getting the best of her, she resolutely set off to explore the rest of the house.

It was beautifully constructed, and Rose knew that this summer, if she was still around, there would be many peaceful hours spent relaxing on that big wrap-around porch. She hadn't noticed any chairs there, but maybe they were stored for the winter in one of the out buildings. A porch like that called for rockers and tables just waiting for a pitcher of lemonade. She could picture sitting there after a full day, resting and enjoying the evening breeze. Beside the lemonade, there would be a plateful of cookies. She'd have to find out Jesse's favorite kind.

"Okay, Rose," she said aloud, giving herself a mental shake. "That's plenty enough daydreaming. When you start wondering about Jesse River's favorite kind of cookies, it's time to direct your thoughts elsewhere. Favorite kind, ha," she snorted, and slid back the pocket doors opening into the front room.

Rose took two steps into the dim room and stopped. A musty, unused odor greeted her, making her nose wrinkle. She wrapped her arms around her waist and ventured further. *Unfriendly, unwelcoming, cold, austere.* The words jumped into her mind. The furniture did nothing to allay the impression. It was large and looked uncomfortable. There was more wood trimming the pieces than cushions. The box-shaped sofa was made up of dark wood curved around a thin, stiff cushion. A stone fireplace took up one wall, long-dead ashes reposing in the hearth.

She stood stock-still on an oval-shaped rug strategically placed in the middle of the room and surrounded by the sofa and chairs. Its once-rich colors now subdued by an accumulation of dust.

Rose made herself take a deep breath and look deeper. The room had possibilities. It could be made beautiful and welcoming. All it would take is a good cleaning, drawing back those heavy ugly drapes to let some sunshine in, doing something with that disagreeable sofa and those horrible chairs, and a cheery fire crackling in the fireplace.

She walked over to the sofa and hesitantly sat down only to get quickly back on her feet. The satin-covered horsehair seat was hard and unyielding. The chairs were of the same material. Not furniture for a tired man to relax on after a hard day's work. It was furniture suitable for . . . Words failed Rose. Then her lips twitched in a mischievous smile. It was furniture fit for a Mr. Whimpstutter or a Mrs. Chinney. She laughed aloud, her voice bouncing back, a hollow, empty sound.

Leaving the room, Rose vowed to herself this would be the first room she'd tackle. "By this time tomorrow night, there will be a fire in that fireplace, comfortable chairs facing it, and a clean welcoming smell in the air. It will be a room in which to spend cold winter evenings and, who knows, maybe even Christmas morning."

That she would be spending Christmas morning in Jesse River's house would never have entered her mind as being anywhere in the realm of possibility.

Chapter 24

Sleep had eluded Rose for long, dark hours into the night. The bed was comfortable, it wasn't that. The room, while needing cleaning, was large and roomy. The view out her window was balm to her rancher's soul, a field that stretched as far as she could see. It was dotted with the reddish brown backs of cattle busily pulling at the grass stubble, their breaths frosty steam in the winter air. If Jesse had sold off the majority of his herd in the fall, there was still a sizeable amount wintering here. Even so, feeding them during the heavy snows Montana was known for could be a challenge.

"I would have given anything to have had a herd even half this size," Rose said quietly, shoving the poor-me thoughts away as she hurried down the stairs.

The house was hushed. All the other inhabitants still sleeping. *Say the name, Rose.*

Jesse. Jesse Rivers.

Now that wasn't so hard, was it?

Hurrying into the kitchen, she shook the grates on the cook stove and the banked embers glowed. Adding wood and opening the damper, she replaced the stove lid and slid forward the coffee pot she'd prepared last night. Shivering in the early morning chill, Rose drew the heavy sweater tighter and blessed the trousers she'd taken to wearing when on her own homestead. Dresses were for afternoon wear when the cold-morning draft didn't whistle up her skirt. Still, she smiled. Jesse's kitchen was sturdy, and even with the stove barely putting out heat, warmer than any she'd been used to. It was a lovely kitchen, made to be the heart of the home, Rose mused as she went to stand in front of the window. Another woman must have loved this room. *I could love this room.* Then she caught herself. *Nonsense. It's not mine to love. But it is mine to enjoy as long as I'm around, doing my job.*

After opening several cupboard doors, Rose found what she was looking for. Standing on tiptoes while stretching above her head, she took down a heavy bowl and began preparing breakfast. Biscuits and gravy. Jesse had said there were sausage links hanging in the smokehouse. She begrudged the time already spent this morning hunting for what she needed and vowed the first order of business would be to familiarize herself with the ranch and arrange the kitchen to her liking. A determined smile flickered across her face as she hurried out to the smokehouse.

By the time she'd finished musing over the front room, it had been too dark outside to look at anymore of the ranch. But, sunshine entered her soul and chased away any doubts. Today was a new day. She'd explore to her heart's content. And, she vowed, she'd pin that elusive Jesse Rivers down and make him tell her what he expected from his new housekeeper. He'd stayed out in the barn long after she'd given up and went upstairs to bed. Tory said Jesse had asked him to tell her he'd catch up with her today and they'd talk. You bet they would!

"Is that coffee I smell?"

Rose had just finished pouring her cup and was busily stirring the sausage gravy when Jesse entered the room. What was there about the man that made the air go still and the room immediately fill with his presence?

Rose nodded. "It is. Sit down and I'll pour you a cup. I'm assuming you don't take cream in your coffee since we don't have any. Now if we—"

"Had a cow. I know, I know," he cut her off with a grumble and just a trace of a smile in his voice.

"Mmm, hmm. And if we had chickens," she said, turning her back to him, "you would have eggs to go with your biscuits and gravy. And fried potatoes," she added. "But since we don't have chickens . . ."

"Miss Bush, starting my morning with coffee I didn't have to make, a warm kitchen that I didn't have to shiver in while I waited for the stove to heat, makes not having cream or eggs a very minor thing. Did I mention the smell of biscuits?" he asked impishly.

Rose ignored the question. "You avoided me last night, Mr. Rivers."

"Huh?"

"We"—she emphasized the word—"agreed that we'd discuss my duties after supper." She placed a heaping plate in front of Jesse, then refilling her cup, sat across from him.

Jesse bent over the plate and took a deep breath. "You getting fired from the school, Miss Bush," he said reverently, "was the best thing that ever happened to me."

"I didn't get fired," she said waspishly, "I quit."

"Hmm," he mumbled around a forkful of fried potatoes. "You always leap before you look?"

"What? Of course I don't. I knew exactly what I was doing. Just what do you mean?"

"Well," he said then swallowed, "seems like you let that temper of yours goad you into quitting without thought as to where you'd live or how you'd manage."

Rose popped to her feet. "Now you listen here, Mr. Rivers. What I do or how I do it is none of your business. You have hired me as your housekeeper but that sure doesn't give you the right to judge me. Five minutes. Five minutes in your company, and I regret saying yes to your offer. But I'm staying. Not because of you—definitely not—but because of the wages you are paying me. Now, if you'll excuse me, I have work to do. Enjoy your breakfast."

"Wait," Jesse called out after her, but her only reply was the sound of her feet clattering up the stairs.

"Well, you handled that well." He frowned, reaching for another biscuit. "I'm sure not making any good grades with the former Teacher Bush. And"—he smiled, taking a large gulp of the best coffee he'd had in ages—"I sure as heck don't want to lose her. Better figure out a way to make amends or the lovely Miss Bush will make my life miserable." But somehow that thought didn't fill him with the worry it should have. Trading words with his new housekeeper was downright pleasant.

Rose slammed the door to her room, taking childish delight in knowing Jesse could hear and feel the reverberations.

Throwing on a heavy coat, she stormed outside, pausing in front of the large barn. Standing there, eyes closed, head thrown back, she took a deep breath of air redolent with the cold breath of winter and the welcome smells only a ranch offered. A smile crept across her face. This was the essence of life.

Jesse found her several minutes later, pitchfork in hand, forking hay to the horses milling about in the corral.

"Hey"—he grabbed the pitchfork—"I didn't hire you to be the ranch hand."

"Let go. Since you haven't had time to tell me exactly what you hired me for, I'll help out where I see help needed. You've got cattle waiting to be fed. Forking hay to the horses is nothing." And to prove her point she gave another large forkful a toss.

"Don't you have plenty to do in the house?" Jesse grumbled.

"Mr. Rivers, your house isn't going anywhere, and from the looks of it, and the accumulation of dust, waiting a few hours more won't cause any major problems. Did you leave Tory enough for his breakfast or do I need to prepare more?"

"Huh?" Her jumping from one thought to another caught him in the middle of a comeback.

"There's plenty," he said shortly. "Tell you what Miss Bush, let's leave me telling you what your duties are alone for a few days and see what happens. You do what you see fit around here, and I'll try to not interfere." He started toward the barn. His parting shot, made through clenched teeth, drifted back on the morning air. "Hell, you'll do it anyway."

As the days wore on, Jesse had to bite his tongue so often he was amazed it wasn't in shreds. He bit it each time he saw Rose taking on one of the heavy or particularly obnoxious ranching chores she seemed to actually enjoy. But darned if it wasn't nice to come in off the range, tired, cold, and dirty, only to find a job he was dreading already done. No matter how much time she spent outside, there was always a hot meal waiting for him. He felt as if his world had been blown in several directions all by Whirlwind Rose, as he'd come to think of her.

Take today, for example. He'd spent the day repairing fencing that cows had broken down and trampled stretching out their long necks, reaching for the elusive clump of dried grass. His back was breaking and every muscle in his arms quivered from trying to dig postholes in the semi-frozen ground. He was cold and in a foul humor, cussing every beef on his ranch. He wanted nothing more than to have a cup of hot coffee and collapse in front of a warm fire. Maybe throw in one of Rose's delicious suppers. He'd been too far out to come back in for the noon meal, and he was hungry as a bear, cranky as one, too. Then he remembered he'd ridden out early this morning, leaving stalls un-mucked, figuring he'd get to them tonight. It was more back-breaking, smelly, dirty work. He'd unsaddled his horse, rubbed him down, and, bent over like an old man, hobbled to the manure filled stalls.

Whirlwind Rose had struck, and each stall was shoveled clean with fresh straw beds. He wandered from stall to stall as begrudging admiration and gratitude filled him. Without him realizing it, Rose had stopped being a thorn in his side, and instead, become the beautiful rose she was named after. She'd weaseled her way in day-by-day, chore-by-chore.

"Of course I appreciate her, who wouldn't?" he muttered, tamping down the growing feelings for his housekeeper. "Appreciation, that's all it is."

"Talking to yourself, Jesse?" Tory asked.

How much had he heard? Jesse turned to him, a scowl replacing the previous softness on his face.

"What are you doing here sneaking around?"

"Sneaking," Tory scoffed. "If you hadn't been questioning and answering yourself, you'd of heard me." Tory shook his head, a sassy grin on his face. "She getting to you?"

"Who?" He was nothing but innocence.

"The person you appreciate."

"You know, Tory, you're not too big for me to turn you over my knee and . . ."

"Oh, yeah? You and what other mule-skinner?" Tory laughed as he danced away from his brother's grasp.

Tory's laughter was a sound Jesse never thought he'd hear again. And he'd been hearing it a lot more lately.

"You'd better save your strength, old man," Tory taunted. "Miss Bush visited the attic today and found the furniture Mom brought with her when she married . . ." His voice faltered. "He wouldn't let her use it. Claimed it wasn't good enough for his fine house. Anyway"—he brightened— "I do believe we will be spending our evening carrying our present furniture up to the attic and bringing back Mom's."

Jesse groaned and cancelled all thoughts of putting his feet up in front of the fire.

"You got to admit, Jesse. She makes us earn every darn piece of pie, cake, or cookie she bakes as a bribe."

"Yeah, she does." He shook his head. "But one bite of that chocolate cake and I'm her slave. What's the bribe tonight?"

"Gingerbread. 'Course she's planning on letting you know there's no cream to put on top since . . ."

"Since we don't have a cow," Jesse added morosely as he put his arm around Tory's shoulders. "Okay, partner, let's go see what the whirlwind has in store for us."

Chapter 25

"There," Rose said, laying the last piece of wood in anticipation of tonight's fire. She surveyed the living room, a smile of satisfaction etched on her face. It was everything she'd hoped for and more.

She'd ordered Jesse and Tory to bed after they'd carried the last chair from the attic. She assured them she was going to bed herself and would finish the room tomorrow. But she didn't. The beautiful grandfather clock, formerly residing dusty and unappreciated in the hall, had struck the half hour after twelve when she'd finally pulled herself up the stairs. She had coerced Jesse and Tory into moving it into the room where it would become an integral, living, presence. Her first thought this morning, before her coffee, before daybreak, had been to creep down the stairs and gaze lovingly at the changed room.

Beeswax and highly polished wood greeted her. All musty odors of disuse were banished, chased away by her dust cloth and broom. The carpet's rich tones reflected on the waxed and polished oak floor. Comfortable sofa and chairs strategically faced the fireplace, calling out a welcome to a weary man, inviting him to let their buttery leather wrap around him. The matching footstool, a beckoning place for feet that had traveled miles since sunup. The flames in the fireplace would lick hungrily at the wood, sending out heat and a rich wood smell.

Rose was glad she'd shooed Jesse and Tory to bed without seeing the completed project. Tonight, they would see it in all its glory. And in the future, she'd serve cups of hot chocolate and thick slices of chocolate cake right here before the fire. Then she'd pick up the basket of mending sitting beside the smaller chair, put her feet up on the crewel embroidered footstool, lean her head back on the chair's pillowy softness and send a silent thanks to Tory's mother for the gift she'd unknowingly given them.

She caught herself. Daydreaming, *that's* what she was doing. Building castles in the air. Painting pictures of a family, a wife, a husband, and a special boy. Well, she wasn't a wife by any stretch of her imagination. And Jesse Rivers, sure as coffee is black, wasn't a husband. With thoughts of coffee, she whirled from the room, softly sliding the door shut behind her.

For heaven's sake, Rose. You're getting maudlin as an old maid. You are the housekeeper. The paid help. And you don't want it any other way." But a small voice in her head asked, "Don't you?"

Hurrying to the kitchen, she began the morning routine of rattling the grates, making coffee, rushing to the smokehouse for ham, and slicing up her last loaf of bread.

"I'll have to add baking bread to the list today. I never saw two men eat like these two." She'd found jars of Emma's jelly in the root cellar and vowed to replenish the jars with jam of her own. "If you are still here, Rose," she admonished.

"If you are still here? What do you mean? Leaving already?"

"Jesse Rivers, I wish you would stop sneaking up on me. It's a nasty habit."

"Not my fault you got caught blabbing to yourself." He grinned at her discomfort and reached for the coffee pot.

"It's not ready yet."

"Huh?"

"I, uh, got a late start."

"Slept in? Abusing my good nature, Miss Bush?"

"I did not sleep in," Rose denied hotly. "And we won't discuss your so called good nature. I was busy elsewhere."

Jesse's eyebrows rose in question.

"It's none of your concern, Mr. Rivers. The coffee has been delayed only moments."

Jesse debated on prodding her more just to see the sparks fly from those blue eyes. The sound of coffee perking against the black lid of the coffee pot stopped him. Wrapping a towel around his hand, he pulled the pot to the back of the stove and wondered if there was any better smell than fresh-brewed coffee on a winter morning, or any morning. Hell, anytime. Then he remembered how good Rose's chocolate cake smelled, and her warm bread just out of the oven, and—he swallowed hard—how good Rose smelled. She carried with her the scent of lilacs, woman, and more times than not, the fresh outdoors.

He shook the thoughts from his mind and poured two cups. "Tory still sacked out?"

Rose nodded. "I think moving all that furniture wore him out." She cracked three eggs into the frying pan, waited a few minutes, then expertly flipped them over, cooking the yolk to a softness Jesse liked. The fact that she already knew many of this man's likes and dislikes escaped her.

"Eggs?"

"Mrs. Watson. As you are well aware, we are dependent on neighbors for eggs and milk."

"You just don't give up, do you, Miss Bush?" he said, taking a big bite of fried egg.

"Not when I'm right."

Jesse bent over the hearty breakfast and concentrated on chewing, swallowing, and ignoring her.

Rose, sensing that her plug for the cow and chickens had hit a sore spot, sat down across from him.

"Mr. Rivers."

"Jesse."

"What?"

"Jesse. My name is Jesse."

"And if memory serves me, it's also Mr. Rivers."

Jesse rolled his eyes in defeat and, pushing his empty plate aside, started to rise.

"Please stay seated. There is something I need to discuss with you."

"Can't it wait? I've got a full—"

"No," she interrupted. "It can't. It's about Tory."

Jesse sat back down and gave her his full attention as a worried frown crossed his face.

"What's the matter with Tory? Is he sick? He was okay last night."

"Nothing's the matter with him." Hesitantly, she took a deep breath. "It's about Christmas."

"Christmas," he spat the word out. "Damn it, Miss Bush, you had me thinking something was wrong."

"Well, it will be if you don't get him something to go under the tree you two are going to cut later this afternoon."

"Tree?"

"Mr. Rivers, you're beginning to sound like an echo. Yes, tree." Her voice grew softer. "Tonight is Christmas Eve. And, it follows that the next day is Christmas. And we"—she fixed him a hard look—"we will be celebrating with a nice dinner, gifts, and a decorated tree. You do have decorations, don't you?"

"How in the hel— Heck would I know?" He uttered the words, then had to drag his eyes away from her pursed lips. Her full, very kissable, pursed lips. Angry at his rebellious thoughts, he snapped out, "I have a ranch to run, and worrying about decorations, or a tree to stick them on, isn't on my to-do list."

"Well, it had better be." Rose glowered. "Tory deserves a Christmas and you, his loving brother," she snapped, "are darn well going to provide it for him. I would suggest you take time from 'running the ranch' and make a trip into town for a few store-bought decorations, and a present."

"Present?"

"There's that echo again. Yes, present. We'll decorate the tree tonight. He'll open his presents tomorrow, Christmas morning." Rose rushed on, not giving Jesse time to interrupt. "And, in the afternoon, we'll go to Wisteria and Ben's for Christmas dinner. Wisteria sent word we're expected. Jarrett and his family will be there, too. That is what families do, and by golly, Mr. Rivers, that is what we'll do. Tory deserves it, and we are going to see he has what he deserves. So, big brother, you'd better get right on those chores. You need to take Tory with you, both for the tree and the trip to town. I'll be busy all day baking."

Jesse couldn't keep the surprise from his face. The whirlwind had swept through his life again. He stumbled to his feet, grabbed his coat and hat, and firmly shut the door behind him.

Rose grinned. "That went well." She bit into a piece of perfectly browned oven toast and washed the bite and the surge of satisfaction down with a swig of coffee.

The Rocking R would have Christmas, or else.

Chapter 26

The house was quiet, and it seemed to Rose as if it were holding its breath, waiting for the spirit of Christmas.

She hummed as she popped the layers of a chocolate cake on a rack to cool. It was wonderful to have the big house and homey kitchen to herself. And if she gave in to letting her mind play the 'what if' game, it would be easy to envision the Rocking R as hers. That was nothing but foolishness. She wasn't a young woman with time for daydreaming. She'd been dealt her role in life, and it was up to her to make the best of this hand.

Jesse had grumbled about having to stop his work and go into town. But when Tory asked him why they were going, a tender look came over his face, and his voice cracked with emotion. He told him there were important things needing done and some of them were secret.

The word 'secret' lit a fire in Tory's inquisitive nature and the questions flowed. Jesse adroitly sidestepped them, and with a saucy wink at Rose, herded Tory out the door.

Rose was turning the handle of the flour sifter when a jingle of harness reins and a muffled, "Whoa" sent her to the front door, dusting her hands across her apron.

Mixed emotions raced through her, regret that her alone time was invaded, and delight in having a visitor. Since her move to the Rocking R, she hadn't seen or talked to anyone but Tory and Jesse. And most of her conversation with Jesse only bordered on talking, more often a verbal battle of wills.

She opened the door and, shading her eyes from the winter sun, gave a whoop of joy.

"Wisteria. What on earth?" Rose ran down the steps. "I didn't expect you. Is something wrong? Why are you here? Of course I'm glad to see you, but . . ."

"Slow down," Wisteria giggled, tying the reins around the buggy's brake handle. "I can only answer one question at a time."

Rose grabbed her sister, gave her a hug, and peered into the buggy. "Where's Robin? Oh, silly question, with Ben."

"Nowhere else, although I have to tell you she was mightily torn. She wanted to come see Aunt Rose, but when Ben started out on his rounds, she quickly changed her mind."

"I'm not at all surprised. Disappointed but not surprised. Now, get to answering my questions."

"I don't get invited inside?"

"Not until you answer the main one. Is everything okay?"

"Yes. All is well in the McCabe household. There is no emergency. I simply wanted to see my sister. The sun may be shining, but the little bit of a wind is cool. Can we please go inside? I can't believe this is winter in Montana and not a drop of snow on the ground, although Ben says that will change any day now."

Rose shepherded Wisteria into the warm kitchen. "I was enjoying the peaceful day, and a visit from you is like icing on a cake. Put your coat over there by the range so it will be warm when you leave. We'll have a cup of coffee and you can fill me in on everything."

"Mmmm, something smells good," Wisteria cried. Then she spied the cooling cakes. "You're doing your Christmas baking, I'll bet."

Rose laughed. "And you'd be right. Jesse and Tory haven't had a real Christmas for far too long. This year, if I have anything to say about it, they will."

Wisteria bent her head, hiding the knowing twinkle in her eye. "So it's Jesse now, is it?"

"What? No, of course not," Rose stammered, flustered.

"It's Mr. Rivers. Did I say Jesse?"

"Mmm, hmm." Wisteria smirked. "You did, and with some feeling, I might add."

Rose pulled herself up straight, coffee pot poised over Wisteria's cup. "The only feeling you might be sensing is for Tory."

"I met the two of them on my way here. Jesse said they were headed to town for some Christmas shopping. Ordered there by the housekeeper. The bossy housekeeper."

A tic formed at the corner of one of Rose's eyes. "He said that. Bossy housekeeper?"

"He did," Wisteria replied, not needing to ask who the 'he' was. She was enjoying this, and was ashamed to admit how delightful it was to see the unflappable Rose squirm.

Rose's lips narrowed. "Well, if I wasn't bossy, Jesse Rivers would ride roughshod over me like I was some . . . some hired hand."

"You *are* a hired hand." Wisteria laughed. "Oh, Rose, give it up. Admit it, Jesse has you . . ."

"Don't you say it, Wisteria McCabe," Rose warned. "I am the housekeeper here. Nothing more. And I certainly don't want it to be anything more."

"If you say so." At a frown from Rose, she sat down and said, "Now, tell me what you've got planned for Christmas at the Rivers' house, and what the two of us are going to bake today. And then I'm going to talk nonstop about Ben, Robin, and Christmas in our new home."

The love beaming from Wisteria's face as she spoke Ben and Robin's names sent feelings of envy surging through Rose. And for the first time, heavy foreboding filled her. A dark possibility that even when she had her own home, her own ranch, there would be an empty spot, a lonely hollow waiting for something she refused to acknowledge.

"If we're going to town, then why are we turning off here?" Tory nodded toward the lane leading to the Watson's ranch. "I just got eggs and milk yesterday."

Jesse couldn't hide the grin from his face. "Christmas is tomorrow."

Tory shrugged. "So?" Christmas had never been a part of his life. He knew today was Christmas Eve, sure, but so what? His mother had given up trying to celebrate in their home after being confronted with his father's threats and scathing comments. He vowed that no such foolishness would take place on the Rocking R. Not on his ranch, not ever.

"Miss Bush is determined we'll have Christmas this year. You and I have been ordered to town to buy gifts and decorations for the tree we're going to cut on the way home."

A look of wonder swept across Tory's face. "A tree? We're going to cut a tree?"

Jesse nodded, unable to hide his foolish grin.

"Presents?"

"Yep."

Tory sat back in his seat.

"You don't like the idea?" Jesse probed, puzzled by Tory's reaction.

Tory shrugged. "Can't remember having Christmas." He turned to Jesse. "I don't know what to do, I mean. Darn it, Jesse, it was just another day of work, and if I got any present, it was maybe the hope that I wouldn't make Dad mad, and he wouldn't be handing out punishment for once."

A haunted sadness flickered in Jesse's eyes. He felt his chest tighten. "I'm so sorry, Tory. It was the same for me." He was at a loss for words and remorse filled him at not being there for his brother.

"Tell you what, we'll just follow Miss Bush's lead. I've only experienced Christmas once and that was so long ago, I don't much know what to do either. One of my fellow ranch hands invited me home with him once, and that was the first time I saw how other people celebrated that special day. It can be wonderful, Tory." Jesse heard the longing in his voice. "Now, what do you think about our saying to hell with all those past, bleak Christmases? Let's make this one so darned good it'll make up for ones missed, starting with this stop at the Watson's."

Tory nodded, pleased to share these feelings and promises with his brother. "Sure, why not? Peers to me we have nothing to lose."

"You may change your mind about that, little brother, when you see what Christmas present I've got in mind for bossy Miss Bush."

Chapter 27

"I can't believe it. You bought a milk cow, her calf, twenty laying hens, and one meaner-than-hel, uh, heck, rooster. Old Man Watson grabbed that money out of your hands while he strutted around asking if you were a farmer now. I wanted to plow my fist into his son's face, and I would have, too, if you hadn't stopped me when he asked if I needed a three-legged milking stool." Then in a falsetto voice, he mocked, "*My sister has one she might sell you.*"

"Any other time, I'd of turned you loose on the little weasel. But we weren't there to teach the Watsons manners. We wanted what they had, and they wanted our money. So a fair trade was made. And you know the best part?"

"No," Tory bit out, still smarting from the teasing.

"Well"—Jesse chuckled—"you don't have to go to the Watsons ever again for eggs or milk."

Tory's face split into a wide grin. "Hey, I never thought of that. Yippee!" he yelled. "Thank you, Miss Bush."

"Don't forget," Jesse admonished, a serious look replacing his grin. "This is a secret. Mr. Watson will deliver the cow, calf, and chickens late tonight. All we have to do is keep Miss Bush out of the barn until Christmas morning."

"Huh? That's all? Now how are we going to do that?"

"You're going to get sick."

"Sick?" The word exploded from Tory's mouth.

"Yep," Jesse said smugly. "Sick. Sick enough you don't want her leaving your side. And knowing Miss Bush, she'll be there doing everything she can to make you well in time for opening presents and dinner at the McCabe's house."

"That's easy." Tory laughed.

"It had better be. Watson said he'd milk the cow before he brings her, but it'll be up to Rose, uh, Miss Bush, to get it done Christmas morning. I just hope Watson can sneak in after dark, like he promised. I'll be out there to meet him."

"Jesse, it ain't gonna work."

"Huh? Why?"

"Miss Bush goes out to the barn right after she puts your breakfast on the table. Lotsa times she's out before you finish eating."

"You just leave all that to me. But you'd better plan getting up earlier than ever so you can be 'sick.'"

"Yeah." The grin filled Tory's face and lit up his eyes.

Later, when Jesse and Tory left the mercantile loaded down with packages, they were laughing and talking nonstop. The fact that there had been few decorations to buy, and most of them were covered with dust, cracked or broken, and outrageously priced, hadn't dampened their spirits. It had been a rare experience, each one trying to outdo the other in keeping secret prospective gifts. They had conspired on Tory's gift to Rose, finally settling on a box of handkerchiefs and a stickpin with a purple stone. The clerk called it an amethyst.

"She'll love it," Tory said, taking it once again out of his pocket and rubbing the setting with his thumb.

"She won't if you rub off all the shine," Jesse teased.

"How come you didn't want to buy her that box of candy? It was a lot better than that book on raising sheep. Sheep," he scoffed.

"Probably," Jesse mused. "But candy is something a guy buys a girl he likes."

"Well, you like Miss Bush," Tory persisted. "Don't you?"

"Sure, just not that way," Jesse said, but the words felt false rolling off his tongue.

"Like a girlfriend?"

"Well, sort of."

"Aww, you shoulda bought the candy." Tory shrugged. "Everyone knows you and Miss Bush are too old to be girlfriend and boyfriend."

Jesse gave Tory a quizzical look but saw his brother was serious. *Well, hell, guess I do seem old to him. Too old to have Miss Bush for a girlfriend, huh? Wouldn't be hard to set him right on that account.* Then he frowned, wondering where that thought came from.

They were in high spirits when they pulled up in front of their house. Jesse sat with the reins looped around his hands, taking in the wraparound porch, the curl of smoke rising from the chimney, the sparkling windows. A feeling of homecoming entered him. Was it only a short time ago he'd seen the house as cold and empty, harboring unhappiness? It wasn't that way at all. In fact, this place was downright welcoming.

"You go on in with what you can carry. I'll put up the team and bring the rest." Jesse needed time to himself, time to analyze the thoughts and feelings that threatened to overwhelm him.

Tory hopped out of the wagon, grabbed up an armful of packages, and with a grin on his face, went up the steps and into the house.

He was a different boy and Jesse knew the reason was a determined, blond-haired woman with sky-blue eyes.

Jesse deliberately dawdled over the evening chores, finally giving in to the lure coaxing him inside the house. Rose. Even her name made him think of something delicate and beautiful. Delicate and beautiful with an underlying strength that Jesse knew he needed and wanted. She'd blown into his life, and when the time was right, she'd blow out. He couldn't allow that.

You can't stop her from leaving. And I don't dare risk it being like father, like son. He opened the door, ignoring the niggling feeling he'd forgotten something important.

The heady redolent smell of things rich and spicy greeted him, wrapping the tantalizing scent around him. It teased his nose and made him pause to take a deep breath. Jesse had to swallow twice as his taste buds responded. Racing up the stairs, he deposited the remaining packages on his bed, then hurried back down, determined to beg a piece, a bite, or a slice of whatever Rose had magically created in the kitchen. Christmas or not, there was a limit to what a man should be expected to endure, especially in his own house.

With that thought in mind, Jesse marched into the kitchen and stopped short. The counter and table were laden with pies, cakes, cookies, and different-shaped breads.

"How on earth did you manage all this in the short time we were gone?" Jesse walked closer to the woman standing in front of the table, a proud smile on her face.

"This?" She swept her hand toward the array of dishes. "Why it was nothing."

"Huh?" Jesse missed the twinkle in her eye.

"Nothing? Lady, there is no way . . ."

Rose giggled, causing Jesse to give her a closer look.

"You're hiding something, Miss Bush."

"Hiding? Why, Mr. Rivers what on earth would I hide?" Innocence blinked from her eyes.

Enjoying her teasing, he shortened the distance between them. There was a plate of cookies directly behind her. Ignoring the fact it wasn't just the cookies tempting him, he playfully reached both arms around her, capturing her, holding her hostage. He swayed closer. He could smell her, a bewitching mingling of scents, sugar, spices, and lilacs. A scent uniquely Rose.

His hands searched behind her back as he leaned in, fumbling for the elusive cookie plate. Suddenly, both of them realized how close he was. How his mouth was only a few inches from hers. How easy it would be to forget all about the cookies and wrap those strong arms around the sometimes irritating, yet uniquely, bewitching woman with the flushed face, the curly, wispy hair, and the very kissable lips.

Jesse bent his head. Rose raised hers. And in the purest of seconds, their lips met, each welcoming the other's as they banished all reasons not to drink of the sweet nectar offered.

She felt so right in his arms. He cupped her face with his large hands and looked deep into her eyes as all sense of time stopped. A door slamming upstairs broke the spell. He uttered a silent curse and forced himself to step back, and turning on his heel, left the room, all thoughts of cookies forgotten. He'd just sampled a confection sweeter than anything a mere mortal could bake.

Chapter 28

With trembling fingers, Rose touched her lips. She closed her eyes as a pleasant shiver ran through her. What had just happened? Jesse Rivers had kissed her, and she'd let it happen. Not just let it happen, but welcomed it.

Rose, what have you done? You foolish woman. First you lose your ranch, then you lose your teaching job, and now you'll lose this position. Despair replaced the exhilaration from being in Jesse's arms. And the kiss. *How will you ever get through the next days, not to mention tonight?*

Well, there's no escape for it, I'll have to leave.

Yes, that's what I'll do.

The decision brought with it a dark cloak that covered her body and seeped into her soul. In the short time she'd been at the Rocking R, she'd come to love it.

I'll leave right after Christmas. I'll have to take advantage of Ben and Wisteria's hospitality. She blinked hard, not allowing the threatening tears to fall. *Maybe it's time to give up. Give up the dream of my own ranch.* And Rose knew once she did, she'd give up a large part of herself. A part that would never resurface.

"Rose?" Jesse stood in the doorway.

She kept her back to him, not wanting him to see the trace of tears still in her eyes.

"Yes," she said, her voice weak. "Do you need something, Mr. Rivers?"

Jesse gave a snort of disgust. "My name is Jesse, Rose. After what just happened, I think we can stop with the Mr. Rivers, don't you?"

Rose gave a deep sigh. "Very well, Jesse." Her tongue faltered over his name.

Jesse thought he'd never heard his name sound so sweet. He straightened his spine and, reminding himself he was his father's son, blurted out what he'd quickly rehearsed in his mind. The words came out gruffer than he intended.

"I owe you an apology. I guess the trip to town, buying presents, seeing and smelling the baking, Christmas, I . . . I lost my head. I made a mistake. It was an impulsive action." He swallowed hard before choking out the next words. "Nothing more." What a lie. It was something more. It was everything, yet it was nothing, nothing he could have. Still, he'd treasure the memory. That, he would have.

"Why, yes, of course," Rose stammered, filled with hurt at his words. "Impulsive. A mistake. Like you said, nothing more."

He touched her shoulder, then, feeling Rose stiffen, jerked his hand back. "Tory and I forgot the tree. We need to go back out and cut one. Uh, would, would you like to come with us?" Longing filled his voice.

Rose wanted to say 'yes.' Wanted it with all her soul. "No," she forced out. "I'm too busy. Way too busy." She stepped back from him. "I've got supper to get, and I planned . . ." Her voice faded.

"What? What did you plan, Rose?"

"Nothing of importance." She skirted past him, escape dominating her thoughts. "You might want to put some logs in the front room fireplace. I finished it last night."

Then she was gone, leaving emptiness behind her.

In that moment, Jesse knew what Rose had planned. She had planned on surprising them with the fire in the newly cleaned and furnished room. Well, he'd ruined that.

"Tory," he bellowed, "meet me in the barn, we've got one more task before supper." He slammed the door behind him.

From her bedroom window, Rose watched the wagon

pull out of the ranch yard. Jesse had made his feelings clear. The kiss was nothing more than a mistake, an impulsive action. Now it was up to her to deal with the consequences of that impulse. He'd apologized. She'd accepted.

"I'll do the same. I'll act as though nothing happened," she said aloud. "I'm the housekeeper, and that's what I'll be until I move on."

Rose tilted her chin and a look of fierce determination filled her eyes. "But I won't stay longer than absolutely necessary. I will make a Christmas Tory will remember. I'll be polite, but reserved, knowing my place. I can do that. I've done harder things. Meanwhile, I'll look for another means of supporting myself. I'll ask Ben and Wisteria to watch for anything, anything at all I can do. Oh, what a fix I've gotten myself into. Now I'm even talking to myself." With those final words, she walked over to the highboy dresser and peered into the mirror held by two curved wooden arms. Her eyes were clear. No sign of tears.

Pleased that decisions had been made, she left the room, banishing all thoughts of the rugged, yet gentle, man who had stolen her heart.

On entering the kitchen, Rose saw the cookies that had tempted Jesse and caught her breath. She skirted the plate as if it were a rattler coiled to strike. Jesse and Tory wouldn't be long. And after supper, they'd decorate the tree. No, she'd retire to her room, and Jesse and Tory would decorate the tree.

With that thought firmly in her mind, she spent the next hour cooking. And if her eyes strayed to the window, hoping to catch sight of a tree-laden wagon, it was only because she didn't want to dish up the meal too soon.

Rose stepped over to the sink and began washing the few dishes in the dishpan. With her hands immersed in the warm, soapy water, her thoughts wandered. The next thing she knew, Tory was shouting outside the front door.

"Miss Bush. Open the door. We need help."

Flinging open the door, Rose found herself met by the tip of an evergreen tree and a grinning boy. Holding up the other end was the man she'd vowed not to think about.

"We got a little carried away," Jesse said, his eyes shining. "Tory just had to have a big one."

"Ha," Tory denied. "You're the one that said we had to have just the right one. You picked this tree. I said it was too big."

"Funny, I don't remember that."

The camaraderie between the two brought a smile to Rose's face.

"Unless you plan on standing there all night arguing, bring it in and we'll see if it will fit in the living room." She threw the door open as wide as it could go.

The tree *was* big. The branches bushed out long and perfect, filling the hall. Brisk winter air merged with the heavy scent of fresh pine, a Christmas smell, and one Rose savored.

Closing the door, she edged past the tree, branches tickling her face, and led the way into the living room.

"Oh, my gosh." She stopped them outside the closed pocket doors. "I forgot. We have to have a bucket for the tree."

"You take my end, Miss Bush, and I'll run to the barn and get one." Not waiting for an answer, Tory thrust his end at her and bolted out the door.

Jesse looked at Rose and both of them burst out laughing.

"I'd say he was a bit excited," Jesse said.

"I'd say you were right," Rose answered. "You push and I'll pull, and we'll see if this giant will fit."

Jesse chuckled. "Sounds like a plan. Once we get it upright, I'll bring in a few logs, and we'll have a tree-decorating party in the new room. And"—his eyes twinkled—"maybe you'd share a few of those cookies? They'd go down real easy with a cup of hot coffee. I thought I'd freeze before Tory quit tramping from tree to tree."

"Cookies it is. I do have supper ready."

"Save it. Let's fill up on cookies and whatever else you might spare from that bakery in the kitchen. We can have supper anytime, but Christmas baking is only once a year."

Rose smiled back at him. All thoughts of not participating in the tree decorating had fled. And, pushed back even further, the thoughts of her leaving.

Laughter filled the room as each decoration was made over and hung. There wasn't near enough decoration to have even one hanging from each branch, but as Tory exclaimed over and over, it had to be the prettiest Christmas tree in the entire state of Montana. She and Jesse wholeheartedly agreed as they teased each other that their side of the tree was the prettiest and best decorated. Plate after plate of cookies was eaten until, finally, the meager decorations had all been hung.

Rose stepped back and happy tears filled her eyes as she glanced around the room. The fire was blazing, sending out waves of warmth and cozy cheer, the furniture beckoned, the waxed floor reflected the glow from the fireplace. It was a beautiful room, filled with people she loved.

Loved? "No, I don't, I can't." Rose didn't realize she'd spoken the words until Jesse turned a puzzled face in her direction.

"What can't you do, Rose?"

"What? Oh," she fumbled, "I, uh, I can't put off doing the chores any longer. What was I thinking of? It's time the animals were fed and . . ."

"Not tonight," Jesse quickly said. "You and Tory take care of the mess we've created and hit the sack. Christmas morning comes early."

Really early. He smiled to himself, thinking of what all he had left to do in the barn. He wanted Rose asleep in her room.

Her room.

Panic swept through him. *Wait. She can't sleep in her room. It has a perfect view of the barn. She'll hear and see Mr. Watson for sure.* Damn, and he'd been congratulating himself on thinking of everything.

Jesse moved behind Rose and jerked his head at Tory. Then he pantomimed rubbing and holding his stomach.

Tory frowned and shook his head.

Jesse rubbed his stomach again and mouthed, "Sick."

Finally, Tory's face cleared and, like a puppet on a string, he bent over and wrapped his arms around his middle.

Chapter 29

"Ooooh, I feel sick. My stomach hurts." Tory gave a loud groan. "Ooooh," he groaned again, even louder.

Jesse made a face and shook his head. Tory was overdoing the groaning and was now doubled so far over he was close to crawling.

Rose ran to his side. "Jesse, don't just stand there, help me get him to the sofa."

Jesse rushed to Tory's side and attempted to guide him to the sofa, but Tory was enjoying every minute of being the star of this play and chose to crumble to the floor, leaving Jesse supporting his full body weight.

"Ooof," Jesse muttered as he grabbed Tory around the chest. "Dang it, Tory, you can help. It's only a few feet to the sofa, you can walk that far." He gave him a hard squeeze that Rose couldn't see.

"Can't," Tory groaned, hiding a grin, "hurts too bad. You'll have to carry me, Jesse."

"What?"

"Jesse, do something. Can't you see he's in pain? Of course he'll carry you to the sofa, Tory." Rose bent over and placed her arm under Tory's legs. "I'll help."

"Oh, hell," Jesse muttered. "I'll get him, Rose. Step back, he's too heavy for you."

"I'll run upstairs and get a pillow and blanket. I'm sure it's all those cookies. If he doesn't improve, you'll have to go for Ben." She flew out of the room, her words trailing behind her.

"Get up, you big faker. If you think I'm lugging you to the sofa, think again. And knock off the groaning."

"Well, I'm terribly sick." Tory moaned again, loud enough Rose heard him upstairs.

He winked at Jesse and fell on the sofa. "Help me, big brother. Maybe if you patted my forehead it would ease the pain."

"I'll ease the pain," Jesse said through gritted teeth.

Rose burst into the room then gently put a pillow behind Tory's head. "Don't just stand there, Jesse, take off his boots." She barked orders, scowling at Jesse to hurry with each task. "Get the dishpan out of the kitchen in case he's going to be sick."

"He's not going to throw up," Jesse snapped, giving Tory a hard look.

"I might," Tory whispered weakly. "Better get the dishpan, Jesse. Hurry."

"Jesse Rivers, whatever is the matter with you? Tory is sick, and you're just standing there like some unfeeling dolt. Now please, do as I ask. It's my fault. I let him eat all those cookies."

"It's not your fault, Rose," Jesse muttered, hurrying from the room after fixing Tory with a narrowed-eye glare.

Returning, he plunked the pan on the floor close to Tory's head.

"Before you go out to do the chores, would you mind getting a pan of cool water and a cloth so I can bathe his face?" Rose asked. "I bet a cool cloth on your forehead would feel good wouldn't it, Tory?"

"It sure would. Jesse, you don't mind, do you? Brother?" Tory said in a faint voice.

"Of course he doesn't."

"No, of course I don't. Why, I'll just trot right in there and get that for you, Lil' Brother. It's the least I can do." He bent close to Tory's ear and in a hot whisper said, "Live it up. 'Cause tomorrow you'll be well and I'll remember."

Tory's eyes flew open and he gave a fearful look at Jesse's retreating back.

"I'll sit by your side until you feel better, Tory," Rose said. "You concentrate on getting better for Christmas tomorrow."

"I'll be fine, Miss Rose. But I do feel better with you beside me."

When Jesse came in from the cold Montana night, Rose stopped him at the living room door. Finger to her lips, she silently motioned him back into the hall.

"He finally dozed off. I don't think we should wake him to go to his own bed, do you?"

"No. If he's asleep, waking him might just start it up again."

"That's what I thought."

"Guess I'll bed down here in case he needs anything." Jesse held his breath.

"No. Before he went to sleep, Tory asked me to stay with him. I'll make a bed in that big chair."

Jesse could have hugged his brother. Maybe he wouldn't get even with him tomorrow after all.

"That doesn't seem right," he weakly protested. "But, if you think you should. Tell you what, I'll get up real early, start the fires, put the coffee on, and see that there won't be any chores to do the rest of the day. I'll make it up to you, Rose."

His gaze held hers as he combed a hand through his hair. It was all she could do not to smooth it back in place.

"I'll make sure the fireplace is banked to last all night. Tomorrow you'll wake up to the smell of coffee and a special day to look forward to. This will be a Christmas no one will forget."

Rose knew she would never forget. If she had nothing else of this man, she'd have her memories.

"I'd better—"

"I'll just go—"

Both spoke at once.

"Go ahead," Jesse said in a gravelly voice. "You were saying . . ."

"I'll just go get some blankets and a pillow."

"Are you sure you'll be okay?"

"Of course. This room is heavenly and that chair just begs to be snuggled in."

Jesse gave a low chuckle. "Like this room, huh? I agree it's a big improvement. Before you came, I didn't realize this house could be anything but a cold, unwelcoming structure. You've made it possible. I just wish I . . ."

He bit off the rest of the words and walked over to the fireplace, struggling with re-gaining control of his emotions.

Rose stood there, holding her breath, an uncertain look on her face. What was he going to say? And how would she have answered if the words had been what she hoped they'd be?

Chapter 30

The wan light of a winter morning crept into the room. Rose stretched and groaned. Blinking to clear the sleep from her eyes and her mind, she drew the blanket tighter around her. What was she doing in a chair in the living room wrapped in a blanket? From the crick in her back, she'd obviously spent the night here. Yawning, she glanced over to the sofa and Tory's sleeping body. Of course, he'd been sick. It was all coming back to her.

Still groggy, she searched through the cobwebs of sleep as an insistent thought tried to break through. What was it? What was niggling at her, demanding acknowledgment? She burrowed deeper into the warm blanket. Suddenly, like a bolt of lightning, she propelled out of the chair. The blanket fell to the floor, unnoticed. Wincing as her foot touched the cold floor, Rose ignored the chill, and a smile took over her face. Today was Christmas. Of course, that was the elusive thought, urging her awake.

"Brrr. It's cold out there." Jesse's voice preceded him into the room. He came over to her chair, a steaming mug of coffee in his hand.

"I promised you'd wake up to the smell of coffee. And I always keep my word."

She took the mug and watched as he went over to the fireplace and added another log.

"I'd rather have the snow than this blasted cold," he said over his shoulder.

"Me, too, especially today." Rose took a sip of the delicious brew. "Mmmm. Perfect."

"Like your coffee, huh?"

She sat back down in the chair, cradling the warmth of the mug in her hands.

"Yes."

"You said 'especially today.' What's so special about today?" he asked innocently as he sauntered over.

"I can't believe it. You've actually forgotten?" Then Rose saw the twinkle in his eye and noticed he was fighting back a grin.

Jesse didn't think it possible, but Rose was even more beautiful this morning. Her hair hung long and thick down her back, not yet restricted in preparation for the day's work. His eyes moved over her and his breathing quickened as he caught a tender expression on her face. If he didn't know better, he'd swear it was a look of— No, he was being fanciful. In a flash it was gone, imagined. Blame it on the early morning, heralding a special day.

"Have you had your coffee yet?" she asked.

"Yep, hours ago. Chores done for the day."

"Then I'll dash upstairs and get dressed. We'll have a big breakfast since we missed supper last night."

"Sounds great. I have to admit, those cookies ran out hours ago."

The warmth that filled him as he stood by her chair wasn't because of the happily burning fireplace. But he couldn't allow himself to ignore the cold fingers of reality accompanying that warmth. Unbidden, his father's angry face, fists raised, loomed before him, and he knew what he was feeling for Rose had to be pushed down, denied and forgotten.

"Jesse." Her voice penetrated the memory. "Are you okay? You have such a strange look on your face. You're not getting sick, too, are you?"

"No, Rose. I'm not sick. Just a touch of reality." And with those cryptic words, he turned away from the desirable woman.

Jesse waited until he heard her leave the room then went over to sofa.

"Wake-up, you big faker," he growled in his brother's ear, giving him a good shake.

"Go away. I'm tired."

"Yeah, well so am I. And I've been up for hours doing all the chores while my poor recovering brother lay in his warm cozy blankets."

"Well, you're the oldest," Tory mumbled, his face pressed into the pillow. "I'm just the little brother who needs his sleep." He dragged the blanket over his head.

"You're right. I'll just go eat that big breakfast Miss Rose is preparing, then come back and sit in front of the fireplace admiring that big tree . . ."

"Christmas." The word and the boy exploded simultaneously. "It's Christmas!" he shouted. Hopping from one foot to the other, he slid on his pants. "You should have gotten me up earlier." Then in a loud whisper, he said, "You haven't already given her the present, the surprise, have you?"

"No, but if you don't lower your voice it won't be a surprise. We'll have to do that right after breakfast. As full as that cow's bag is, she's going to need milking sooner than I thought. That is, unless you know how to milk?" He grinned wickedly.

"Huh? Not on your life. Anyway, Rose'd be mad if we didn't let her do the first milking."

"Yeah." Jesse laughed. "And aren't we lucky that's the truth of it?"

"Let's forget breakfast and give it to her now," he wheedled, slipping his shirt over his head and stumbling toward the door.

Rose was entering the room and quickly stepped to the side. "Careful, Tory. Would it be safe to say you are over any sickness and know what morning this is?" She paused, then asked, "Give what to her now?"

"Huh?" Tory's mouth hung open as he grasped for answers.

"Feet that big shouldn't be put in one's mouth," Jesse muttered, giving Tory a push. "Let Rose go first and we'll . . ." He took a deep breath, his mind racing for a way to cover the blunder, something, anything. ". . . strike a bargain with her," he blurted.

Rose raised her eyes to the tall man. "A bargain?"

"Sure," Jesse fumbled. "A bargain. How about, since it's Christmas, Tory and I will do the dishes and clean up after that big breakfast you're going to cook. How's that for a—a bargain?"

Rose's eyebrows drew together as she looked from man to boy. "I guess. Sure, that's fair."

"Well it don't sound fair to me," Tory said loudly, following Rose into the kitchen. "Come on, Jesse. I can't wait. Let's do it now."

"After breakfast." Jesse ground the words through clenched teeth. "It can wait until after breakfast."

"No, it can't." Tory's face was a contradiction of stubbornness and excitement.

"Stop right now." Rose held up a hand, silencing the two. "What is this all about? I refuse to have my Christmas morning ruined with bickering."

"Yeah, Jesse, you're ruining her Christmas morning." Tory gave him a superior smirk.

Rose turned her face expectantly to Jesse, her blue eyes piercing.

"Okay," Jesse said resignedly. "My stomach's rubbing my backbone, but what the heck. Rose, get a heavy coat on. You too, Tory."

"A coat?" Rose asked. "Whatever for?"

"Rose," Jesse said in a low beleaguered voice, "just do as I ask, okay? No more questions."

Tory ran to the porch and started grabbing coats off the pegs.

He threw them at the two adults, struggling into his, then jerked open the door and stepped into the cold Montana dawn.

Chapter 31

Rose stopped so suddenly Jesse stumbled into her. She raised her face to the sky, her eyes closed in ecstasy.

His large hand fell across the middle of her back, steadying her.

"Whoa. I about knocked you over."

"Oh, Jesse, look."

He did, but not up at the sky. Rose's face was damp and minute crystals winked on her eyelids. His breath caught, and he knew this day, this woman, would be forever etched in his memory.

"Snow," she breathed softly. "It's snowing." She flung her arms upward and, laughing, whirled around, catching the wet flakes on her tongue.

"Snow for Christmas," she said. "Nothing can top this. Absolutely nothing. I wished so hard for snow. Now I have everything I want to make today perfect."

"You think so, huh?" His heart filled to bursting as he pulled her to him. "Well, Tory and I have something to show you that just might change your mind."

"Nope. Couldn't." She gave a happy skip as he urged her toward the open barn door and an impatiently waiting Tory.

"Jesse, make her close her eyes," Tory shouted.

"You heard the man, er, boy. Close your eyes."

"My eyes? Whatever for? If I close my eyes I might . . ."

With trembling fingers, Jesse placed them on each of her eyelids and gently closed them. "There," he whispered. "Now give me your hand. Keep them shut. Trust me."

Rose knew at that moment she loved Jesse Rivers and trusted him with her heart. If only he felt the same way.

Tory grabbed Rose's other hand, breaking the spell cast between the two.

"No peeking, Miss Rose. Not until Jesse and I say you can look."

Rose chuckled. "I won't. I promise."

Sounds greeted her as she was led farther into the barn. Sounds and warmth. What was it? She closed her eyes even tighter and willed herself to recognize what her ears were telling her.

"Chickens," she squealed. "There's chickens and . . . and a rooster. Can I look?" she begged. "I'm opening my eyes."

"Not yet." Tory slapped his palm across her eyes. "Darn chickens," he grumbled.

"Tory, it's okay." Jesse laughed. "Let her look."

Reluctantly, he removed his hand.

Rose's eyes snapped open, and she turned toward the cages of chickens angrily letting them know that being penned up wasn't their idea of a good morning.

"You bought chickens. Thank you, thank you. I love this surprise. Tory, you were right. It couldn't wait. We have to build them a hen house." Just then the rooster gave out another loud crow. "Oops," she chuckled. "I should say chicken house. Until then, they'll have to stay in the barn. Can we fence off an area so they can get out of those little pens?" Rose was firing off questions and talking so fast, she missed the nod Jesse gave Tory over her head.

"Miss Rose . . ."

"Rose, Tory. Please call me Rose when there's just the three of us. But, you will need to call me Miss Rose when we're around others," she admonished distractedly.

The three of us. The words tore at Jesse.

"There's more Miss, uh, Rose." Tory gave her hand a tug leading her over to an enclosed paddock.

"More?" She laughed. "What more could there be? There must be at least twenty chickens here."

"Twenty-five," Jesse mumbled, his voice hoarse with emotion. "Twenty-five, but Tory's right. There is more." He opened the paddock door.

The milk cow turned her head at the sound, and gave them an inquisitive look as if to say, "Who are you?" Her big brown eyes, full of expression, peeked out from under long black lashes. Then she blew through her nose, and went back to the more important task of munching her hay, not at all perturbed at sharing her stall. Her tail swished back and forth, swatting at imaginary flies as she shifted from one foot to another, her full bag swinging between bony hips.

"No." The word exploded from Rose with a gush of air. "No, it can't be."

"Well, it sure is," Jesse said with a grin.

"A milk cow," Rose whispered, reaching out to run her hand across the cow's smooth hide. Then she turned to the waiting man and boy, tears streaming down her face. "You bought me a milk cow. You-You bought me a Christmas present."

Jesse folded her into his arms. "Hey, we didn't mean to make your cry. Don't you like her? 'Cause if you don't we can probably take her back . . ."

"Don't you dare, Jesse Rivers. I-I love her." She brushed her hand across her face. "These are tears of joy, silly. Come here, Tory, I need to hug you."

Red-faced, Tory moved closer.

Rose threw her arms around the boy then stretched them even more to include the watching man.

"Thank you so much. Oh, darn, I'm going to cry some more."

"You're welcome, Rose," Jesse said huskily. "She's yours, and that fellow waiting for his bucket of milk is yours, too."

"A calf?"

"In the next stall."

Rose's hand flew to her mouth. "This is the best present I've ever had. The best Christmas ever. How on earth did you two sneak this all in without me knowing?" Then a glint entered her eyes and she put her hands on her hips in mock displeasure.

"You tricked me. You weren't sick at all, were you, Tory? All that groaning and clutching your stomach, it was just an act."

Tory grinned, unashamed at being found out. "We had to think of some way to keep you from looking out when Mr. Watson delivered them last night."

"I ought to beat both of you. I was worried to death. I almost sent for Ben, thinking you were seriously ill."

"Sorry," Tory chortled.

"Yeah," Jesse echoed.

"No, you're not. You two aren't sorry at all. And"—Rose's smile grew even wider—"neither am I. Cream, milk, and eggs. We'll never have to depend on the Watsons again."

"Like I said, Rose, they're yours. The start of your herd for your ranch. When you leave, they go with you."

When you leave.

The words hung between them, casting a pall on the celebrating.

Unaware of the charged emotions, Tory piped up, "Well, I'm ready for that big breakfast. I'm starving."

"Not so fast, mister. We're looking at a cow that needs milking and chickens that need out of those small pens." Rose cast her eyes around the area. "No milk bucket, no stool, no stanchion." A look of dismay crossed her face.

Jesse stepped out of the paddock, returning with a shiny new milk bucket in one hand and a three-legged stool in the other.

"We bought the bucket in town, and Tory coaxed the stool away from Mr. Watson's daughter."

"Yeah, and you can't imagine the ribbing I got." Tory gave them a wounded look.

"You two have thought of everything," Rose said softly, her eyes pooling once more with tears. She took the stool and bucket from Jesse's hands.

"Watson said she was an easy milker. He claims she stands there while you do the job," Jesse said.

Rose shook her head as she placed the bucket under the cow and gingerly sat on the stool.

"Jesse." Her quiet voice floated softly over her shoulder as the sound of milk pinging against the side of the bucket filled the air. "You are like no man I've ever known. Arrogant, sarcastic, bossy, and"—her voice faltered—"thoughtful and wonderful. So very wonderful."

Chapter 32

"Oatmeal and burned toast? On Christmas morning? Where's that big breakfast I was promised?" The look on Tory's face was one of total disgust.

Jesse glared at him. "Out in the barn fussing over the Christmas present you just couldn't wait until we ate to give her."

"Well, I didn't think she'd be so batty over a bunch of dumb chickens and a cow. And"—Tory frowned, pushing the full bowl aside—"I didn't think I'd ever have to eat another of your attempts at cooking." He ruefully eyed the burnt toast.

"Yeah, and I didn't think I'd have to listen to your complaining either."

Rose stood at the kitchen door, hand on the knob, listening to the angry words batted back and forth. When she'd heard enough, she stepped inside and set the full pail of milk on the counter then turned to the two people she'd come to love. Smiling to herself, she took in the scowls on both of their faces.

"Stop your scowling," she ordered with mock severity, looking from one to the other. "It's Christmas."

"Well, I'm still hungry," Tory whined.

"Eat your oatmeal then," Jesse barked.

"Yuck." Tory gave the bowl another shove.

"Tory, please quit complaining long enough to go to the cellar and bring me two gallon jars. This milk has to be strained before we drink it."

When he returned, Rose rinsed the jugs and, taking a thin white dishtowel, spread it over the mouth of one of the jars.

"Need help?" Jesse came over to her side.

"Yes. If you'll keep the cloth pulled tight, I'll slowly pour the milk over it and into the jar. That way, we'll catch any impurities. Once we've done that, it'll go to the spring house to cool, and by tomorrow there will be thick, rich cream to skim off the top. Just think, we'll have our own butter and cream for baking." She clapped her hands in glee. "Jesse, we'll have cream for anything we want to use it for or put it on."

Jesse smiled. Rose's joy was contagious. It was easy to get caught up in her delight over what appeared to him more work for an already busy woman.

"And," she said, her eyes sparkling, "when we're finished here, we'll go into the living room. I'm sure I saw presents under that tree. Tory, you won't starve before we leave for Christmas dinner at Ben and Wisteria's. I can assure you there will be so much to eat, you'll swear you'll never be able to eat again."

"Hey. Yeah. Presents. I forgot. Come on, you two." He charged into the living room.

Rose and Jesse looked at each other and laughed.

"Tory," Jesse called, "put another log on the fire. We'll be finished here in a minute."

Rose turned to Jesse. "You did get him something, didn't you?"

"No, why would I?"

"You didn't?" Rose's blue eyes widened. "Jesse, how could you?"

"Guess I forgot I was supposed to." And the grin he'd been fighting spread across his face.

Rose doubled up her fist and slugged him in the arm.

"Now why'd you do that? You could hurt a person." Laughter danced in his eyes.

Rose rubbed her knuckles. The muscles in Jesse's arm were rock hard. "Yes, and the person would be me," she said. "That's for lying and scaring me."

"You know, since you've become a rancher, you've gotten mighty bossy. Having your own herd has gone to your head." Jesse liked nothing more than to provoke her quick flashes of temper.

"Hush. Pay attention to what you're doing. Hold that cloth tight." Then she asked, "Tory's really enjoying today, isn't he?"

"Thanks to you, he enjoyed yesterday and today." Jesse shook his head, chuckling. "Had you going with that stomachache though, didn't he?"

"That was mean." But her happy laugh made a mockery of her words.

When the milk was put away, they joined Tory in the living room and found him sitting cross-legged in front of the tree, a present in his hands.

"About time. Here, this is for you, Jesse." Tory's face was a mixture of apprehension and excitement as he handed his brother a long, narrow package.

"Thank you, Tory. It's a shame I didn't think to get anything for you."

"You didn't? Uh, that's okay." He shrugged, trying to hide his disappointment.

"Jesse Rivers, you stop that right now," Rose scolded with mock severity.

"Well, I might have forgotten. I've been awfully busy buying cows and chickens."

"Aww, I knew you didn't forget." But the relief in his voice said differently.

Jesse winked at his brother and swallowed hard. Today couldn't get any better. Maybe with more days like today, the past would be forgotten and they'd both heal.

Jesse tore the brown paper from the box, set it aside, and gently removed the lid. He looked at the object nestled there, blinked, and, biting his lips, looked away.

"I didn't put it on our account, Jesse," Tory said worriedly, watching Jesse's reaction. "I'm going to do some chores at the mercantile until it's paid for. They, uh, they said there was plenty for me to do. I won't forget I have chores here, too. I won't."

Jesse hooked an arm around Tory's neck and pulled him into his chest. "Tory, I wasn't worried. I was overwhelmed. I've never had a Christmas gift before, but I can't imagine anything better than this knife."

Tory stepped back and looked into his brother's eyes. "You really like it?"

"I really like it," Jesse said hoarsely. He cleared his throat, "I really like it." He lifted the knife from the box. It wouldn't have been handled any more carefully had it been solid gold.

"Mr. Benson said it was real good for doing heavy work."

"That it is." Jesse carefully ran his thumb along the four-inch fixed blade. "Sharp little dickens." He chuckled, giving it a jiggle. "Doesn't weigh much."

"Is that good?" Tory asked, his brow wrinkling.

"Sure is. That's a sturdy leather handle." Jesse turned the knife over in his hand, his smile widening. "Tory, this is about seven inches of fine craftsmanship. It's a knife to be proud of. First thing tomorrow, we'll make a leather sheath for it." He gave Tory another crushing hug.

"Aw." Embarrassed, Tory pulled away. "It wasn't nothing."

"Tell you what, kid, if that's nothing, you can give me nothing every Christmas. Now, how about you open your present from me?"

"Gosh, this Christmas thing is great." Tory tore into Jesse's package, ripping off the paper covering a hinged, wooden box. He turned the small clasp and opened the lid. "Paints," he whispered. "Brushes," he said in another whisper. "There must be fifty colors. I've never seen this many paints."

"Oh, Tory," Rose said, smiling. "You have every color needed to bring your plants and flowers alive." Then she handed him her gift. "This will be a good companion for your paints."

With more restraint, Tory removed the wrapping and held a thick book in his hands. "Miss Rose, this is your botany book."

"*Was* my botany book, Tory. Now it's yours. You're the botanist, and by rights should have a resource manual."

Tory gave a big sigh. "Thanks, Jesse, Rose. I'll never forget today." He started to re-wrap the paints when a small slip of paper fell out. It was an advertisement from a mail order catalog. Slowly, Tory read the words, then looked up at Jesse.

"It's an advertisement for a Botany Field Kit. '*Everything a botanist needs for collecting and documenting specimens,*' he read aloud.

"Mr. Benson ordered it for me. Sorry you have to wait," Jesse said softly.

"Sorry," Tory exploded. "Well, I'm not sorry. This is a kit a real botanist uses."

"Well, Tory," Jesse mumbled, "to me you are a real botanist. I couldn't be prouder."

Awkward with emotion, both brothers grabbed the other's hand and squeezed.

"Okay, you two, I refuse to cry anymore on Christmas Day," Rose interrupted. "Jesse, here's my gift."

"Darn it, Rose. I don't have anything under the tree for you."

"Well, why should you? The best gift ever is out in the barn clucking and munching hay."

Jesse pulled a book from behind his back. "Here."

"I thought you said you didn't have anything under the tree for me?" Rose chided.

"It's not under the tree, now anyway." Jesse's face broke into a grin. "Hope you like it. I didn't wrap—"

"You didn't have to. Oh." Her eyes widened. "It's a book on raising sheep." She shook her head. "I've vowed never again to put all my eggs in one basket. I planned to raise sheep as well as beef. Thank you so much, Jesse." She shifted toward him as though to thank him with a hug, then pulled back.

A look of disappointment crossed Jesse's face. He lowered his head, concentrating on the gift in his hands. "Is it good to eat?" He tried to joke.

"Absolutely not."

Jesse laid aside the paper and took out a hand-knitted scarf. "It's beautiful." He ran his large, work-roughened hands down the soft wool.

"It's brown with flecks of green. Like your eyes." Mortified at what had slipped out, Rose started gathering up the discarded paper. "I'll just take this into the kitchen. We'll have to be leaving before long for Wisteria and Ben's." She hurried out of the room, not seeing Jesse's gaze follow her.

Chapter 33

The months passed, leaving Christmas a fond memory. Rose and Jesse skirted around each other, both denying feelings too frightening to acknowledge.

Spring was magical in its fresh awakening. Tender shoots of grass shot up, and heifers dropped healthy calves. It was as if the ranch was basking in the peace that had settled over it. Jesse worked from early morning light to dusk, coming in tired, but happier than he ever imagined. Tory worked beside him and Rose often joined them doing her share and more. And if she and Jesse's eyes often met and rested on each other, it was only mutual pleasure in what they were doing. Of course it was.

The only black cloud on the horizon was when Rose remembered her vow to leave come spring. More and more, she saw traits in Jesse to admire. He would be so easy to lean on. His strength, tempered with gentle kindness, set him apart from other men she'd known. His firm guidance was turning Tory into a confident young man. And, with each passing day, the time came closer. It was painful to care so much and know that it wasn't returned.

Jesse was aware a struggle was going on inside of Rose. Too often he caught a faraway look in her eyes. But he was fighting a battle of his own. He refused to name what he felt each time he glanced up and saw this beautiful woman with hair that gleamed like gold and eyes that shot back dark blue shards of life. He relived her chuckle of joy as she watched her calf kick up its heels and run a tight circle under its mother's watchful eye. The combination of spring air and warm sunshine brought out an exuberant feistiness. Against his will, he lay in bed at night seeing her, smelling the scent of lilacs she carried with her, and hearing her soft laughter when he teased her about naming her milk cow Holly.

"Holly, what kind of name is that? I suppose if I'd given her to you for Easter, you'd name her Bunny."

The thrill he experienced seeing her at day's end had become painful. Rose's ready smile made problems melt away and tired muscles relax. His mornings started with him eagerly dressing and going into the kitchen, finding her looking like an angel, as she gave him a sweet "hello" and handed him a mug of coffee. Rose was becoming his life's breath and he fought hard against it.

Each time he saw her avidly reading the book on raising sheep or filling paper with innumerable columns of figures, a cold dread clutched him. Rose would be leaving. And she'd take the sunshine with her. Her drive to have a ranch of her own hadn't lessened.

Tory knew it, too. "Jesse," he said one afternoon when they were repairing fencing, "what are we going to do when Rose leaves us?"

The question caught him by surprise. He gave his full attention to nailing the wire to the post he'd just set in the rock hard ground while he searched for an answer. It was a question he'd asked himself many times. He removed his gloves and wiped his arm across his brow.

"I don't know." He'd debated on answering as if her leaving or staying made no difference. But, honesty won out. He expected honesty from Tory and owed him the same.

"Do you care?" Tory's eyes bored into Jesse, daring him to respond falsely.

Jesse cleared his throat and picked back up the hammer and a handful of nails. With unnecessary force, he banged the nail into the post, making that his answer.

"Jesse, do you?" Tory asked with the persistence of youth.

"'Course I do," Jesse snapped in a low, gravelly voice.

"Then why don't you do something about it?" he asked, an accusing hint of anger in his words.

"Damn it, Tory, just what would you suggest I do, lock her in the root cellar?" He grabbed another strand of loose wire and with frustrated strength, pulled it tight. His muscled forearm bunched as he drove the nails.

"Hey, you'll knock the post over hitting it like that." Tory glared at him. "And, no, I don't expect you to lock her in the root cellar," he said sarcastically.

"Yeah," Jesse growled, "then what do you expect?"

"I expect you oughta marry her, that's what."

Jesse whirled around, his fist white as it gripped the hammer. "What did you just say?"

"You heard me, Jesse. I said you should marry her. That way she'd have a ranch. We could divide it three ways." Tory followed the words with a smile, as if pleased with his rationalization. "She likes it fine here."

"Oh yeah, Mr. Know Everything, what makes you so sure of that?" Jesse held his breath, needing to hear something reassuring.

"I heard her tell Miss Wisteria she loved this place and how she hated to leave."

"Tory, if she was so all-fired sad and hating to leave, she wouldn't. Ranch or no ranch."

"Well, I still think you should marry her."

"There's more to marriage than that." Jesse shook his head and drove another nail deep into the post. "Lots more," he added with vehemence.

"What?"

"Love. There has to be love. I've seen marriages without it, and it's not a pretty thing. You have too," he said as an afterthought.

Tory hung his head. "Yeah, my mom and our dad. They didn't love each other."

"Maybe at one time they did, Tory. But our dad ruined whatever feelings your mother had for him. It doesn't take much temper and fists to kill love. You and I both know that."

Neither one spoke, and the spring day took on a heavy stillness.

Jesse faced Tory. "I couldn't do that to her," he said softly, "no matter what I feel. How do I know I wouldn't handle things the same way? How do I know I wouldn't let anger fill me with a red haze until I'd strike out at the one person I love?" That he'd used the present tense was lost on him.

"Do you love her, Jesse?"

"Huh?"

"Rose, do you love her?"

"I don't dare love her."

"Then we'll lose her." Tory's voice was flat, filled with helplessness.

Jesse nodded. "I expect so."

Chapter 34

Rose was in the barn, helping Jesse and Tory clean stalls when a wagon rumbled into the yard. Ben sawed back on the reins and the frisky mare came to a stop proudly tossing her head.

Ben grinned and called out, "Hey, you three. Got anything cold for a tired doctor? I've been up all night setting a broken arm and leg over at the Watson's place. Never heard such carrying-on. Mrs. Watson begged me to stay the night and gave me cup after cup of the vilest coffee I've ever tasted." He walked toward them while speaking. "I'm dry to the bone. Fed her plant most of my coffee when her back was turned." He chuckled.

"Watsons? Mr. Watson?" Jesse asked.

"Nope, that boy of theirs. The oldest one. Fell out of a tree. I shouldn't say it, but if he'd landed on his head, he'd probably have been okay."

Tory let out a whoop. "All right. Yippee!"

"Tory," Jesse and Rose admonished, not daring to look at the each other.

"Well, it couldn't have happened to a . . ."

"Tory," Jesse said quietly. "That's enough. We don't rejoice over someone else's misfortune." Then he turned away, unable to hide his grin. "Even if the little brat deserved it."

"Yeah." Tory slapped his brother on the back, then caught Rose's eye. "I mean, yeah, that's too bad all right. Yep, too bad."

"Shame on you two." Rose coughed, her hand covering the smile on her lips. "I'm sure he's in pain. Tory, maybe you'd like to take your friend over some of those gingersnaps I baked yesterday. Yes, that would be a nice thing to do. I'll get them ready and Jesse can drive you over." She folded her arms across her chest, daring either one to say anything.

"Aw, Rose," Tory started only to be stopped by Jesse's elbow in his ribs.

"Yes, Tory?"

"Uh, nothing. I'd be"—he choked on the word—"happy to take the cookies. Glad you thought of it."

"Of course you are," she said sweetly. "Ben, please come into the house and I'll give you a glass of lemonade and a plate of those cookies. Or, maybe you'd like a slice of cherry pie with a dollop of sweet cream on top?"

Leading the way into the house, she missed the knowing look and wink between the three smiling people following her.

"Actually," Ben said between bites of cookie and swigs of lemonade, "I was planning on driving out to see you today, Rose."

"You were? Is everything okay at home? Wisteria, Robin?"

"They're fine," he hastened to reassure her.

"Need help with something, Ben?" Jesse asked, reaching for another cookie.

"As a matter of fact, I do." He looked fully at Rose. "I need your assistance, Rose."

"Mine?"

He nodded. "I have a patient, a very difficult patient," he added, "who is refusing to let me examine her."

Rose furrowed her brow. "Why?"

Ben smiled. "Because I'm a man. Her husband went against her will to ask me to see her. I tried, but could only get as close as a blanket pulled up to her chin. She admitted to nausea, extreme tiredness, and unable to keep anything down. This was all told with tears rolling down her face. Her husband is beside himself and both are convinced she has a life-threatening illness."

"Does she?" Rose asked.

"I don't honestly know. It was all I could do to get her to tell me that much. As for touching her, absolutely not."

"And you think I could help?" Rose gave him a puzzled look. "I'm no nurse, Ben."

"I know. But I can't ask Aries. Jarrett would have a fit if I suggested her riding into town. The baby's due any day." He chuckled. "My brother's like an old hen, clucking around her, afraid to let her out of his sight. And Ted's busy keeping Angelique out from under foot. It's a wild household right now. The only sane one is Tim. He's trying to take on most of the chores so Jarrett can hover."

Rose's eyes were filled with laughter as she said, "I don't need you to tell me why you can't ask Wisteria. For a doctor's wife, she's awfully squeamish. I'm afraid you'd have two patients if she accompanied you."

"I would. That's a fact." An indulgent smile crossed his face and his eyes filled with love. "Wisteria makes no excuses for her weak stomach. I'd send Robin if she was a few years older."

"She could do it, I have no doubt. By the time she's five, she'll be doing surgery." Rose's words brought a chuckle from everyone.

"Would you be willing?" Ben asked. "I'll pay you."

"That's not necessary, Ben. Of course, I'll do it."

"That's a relief. And I will pay you," he said forcefully. "Because with Aries unable to do her part for the next few months, I may be asking for your assistance quite often."

He glanced over to Jesse, surprised at the frown on the man's face. "Something wrong, Jesse? Would you rather Rose didn't help? I'd make sure it didn't interfere with her duties here."

Jesse forced enthusiasm into his answer. "No, of course I don't care. Knowing Rose, I'm sure nothing will go amiss here." He rose to his feet. "Come on, Tory, let's get those cookies delivered. We'll leave you two to work out the details. Ben, good to see you again. Christmas dinner is long time past. We need to get together again soon." He shook Ben's proffered hand, and with Tory following him, left the room. He hadn't yet closed the door when the doctor's next words hit him like a hammer.

"The money will help you get your ranch that much quicker, Rose."

Chapter 35

"Ben, you're being awfully mysterious about this patient." Rose shifted position on the wagon seat. "Don't you think I should at least know her name? We're coming into town, and I feel like I'm purposely being kept in the dark. You've skirted around every question I've asked."

"Guess I have been evasive." He smiled at the lovely woman sitting beside him. As tired as Ben was, they'd both decided to make the first call on the sick woman today. Jesse and Tory wouldn't be back from the Watson for a while, and Rose had put a stew on to simmer that morning. She'd be home in plenty time for supper.

"I sure appreciate Jesse loaning you to me." He stalled again.

Rose looked off into the distance, busy mulling over something she wanted to share with her kind and understanding brother-in-law. Making up her mind, she turned to him, her voice low.

"Ben, do you know much about Jesse?"

He shook his head. "No, I've only known him a short time. Jarrett knows him better than I do. Why?"

"I'm being silly, but—" She paused, wishing she hadn't started the conversation. "It's nothing, I shouldn't have bothered you."

Ben pulled back on the reins, stopping the wagon. "You're not bothering me. I've felt you had something on your mind since we left the ranch. What is it? Are you regretting helping me?"

"No," she protested loudly. "Of course not. I'm grateful you asked. It's just Jesse seems . . ." Rose sighed, not daring to look at him.

Ben touched her chin and gently tipped her face toward him. The tears in her eyes surprised him as she quickly brushed them away.

"Rose, you're in love with him, aren't you?"

"Yes," she whispered.

"And he . . .?"

"He doesn't know. He doesn't feel the same way."

Ben gave a snort of laughter. "Oh, yes he does. I've caught him looking at you. It's like he's drinking in every drop, storing it away. He cares."

"No. He doesn't. When I mention my ranch and leaving as soon as I save enough money, he clouds up and walks away. My leaving would simply be an inconvenience."

"You're wrong, Rose. Jesse's had a hard life. As I understand it, his father beat him quite often. He experienced the man's explosive anger and watched it destroy his mother. If I were to venture a guess, I'd say he's afraid to love."

"Afraid?" Rose tried to keep the hope out of her voice. Could Ben be right? Did Jesse really care for her, but was afraid to let her know?

Ben jiggled the reins, starting the horse into a trot, "I would be. If I were Jesse, I'd hold back my love. He's never been a part of a happy home until you came. And like everything else he's known, it's temporary. You'll leave, and again he'll have nothing. So he's determined not to care, not to hurt. And, maybe, not to be his dad."

"He's nothing like his dad. Jesse would never be mean to someone he loved. You should see him with Tory. There have been times I wouldn't hold it against Jesse if he gave him a good shake. But he doesn't. He takes time to reason with him, to talk and listen. I can't imagine him ever using his fists on a woman or child. I'm not saying he would back down from a fight, but he wouldn't provoke one. The other man would have to initiate it."

Ben smiled at the vehemence in her voice. She was protective of Jesse, ready to defend him against anyone that maligned him. Jesse Rivers was a lucky man. But if he was right, Jesse would have to be pushed into admitting his love.

"Have you told him how you feel?"

"Of course not. I couldn't possibly . . ."

"You'll just leave and lose the chance at sharing life with a man you love. Is that ranch worth it?"

"No," she said softly. "I'd give it up in a minute for him and Tory. They've become as vital to me as breathing."

"Then, Rose, fight for him."

"What if he doesn't care? What if you're wrong?"

"I'm not. Jesse loves you, but there's something stopping him from allowing himself to act on that love. It will take a strong woman to overcome that." He turned toward her. "And you're a strong woman, Rose."

A smile touched her lips. "I am. I just hope I'm strong enough to not be humiliated if I try and fail."

"Better to try than leave and always wonder."

Rose chuckled. "How'd you get to be so smart, Ben McCabe?"

"Years of making mistakes." He pulled back the reins, halting the horse in front of a white house with a wide porch and picket fence surrounding it. There were two chairs placed on the porch, looking as if no one ever used them. In fact, the house had a pristine, cold look about it.

"Who lives here, Ben? Our patient?"

Ben nodded just as the front door slammed open and Willy Backley bounded down the stairs.

"Doc, Ma's fierce sick. She's been puking up her food."

"Willy, that'll be enough." A thin, stoop-shouldered man followed the boy down the steps.

"I'm just telling him about—"

"I know what you're telling him, son, and like I said, that'll be enough."

Ben climbed out of the wagon and offered his hand to Rose.

"Ben," Rose said between clamped teeth, "this is Mrs. Backley's house."

"It is," Ben muttered, still holding out his hand.

"Then Mrs. Backley is . . ."

"My patient," Ben gulped.

"You tricked . . . I'm not—" Her words were cut off by Mr. Backley coming to the side of the wagon.

"We sure appreciate your coming, Doc. Especially after the way Mother refused to let you exam her. Is this the nurse you were telling us about? She seems awfully young. I'm not sure Mother will . . ."

"Mr. Backley, this is Rose Bush, and 'Mother' will either let her help with the examination, or I'll walk out of here and there will be no medical help available. Unless you want to drive close to one hundred miles looking for a doctor." Ben's voice was harsh. "Now, I'm a busy man and Miss Bush has graciously agreed to assist me, although I had to be less than honest to get her here. Your wife wasn't the kindest woman to Rose."

Mr. Backley's face turned red as he put everything together. He knew all about the infamous Miss Bush. Hadn't his wife ranted and raved about her for days?

"Dad"—Willy pulled at his arm—"Miss Bush ain't no nurse. She's a schoolteacher."

"Willy, you scat. Now I won't be telling you again." He emphasized his words with a pop to Willy's behind. "And don't you come back until you hear me call for you. Understand?"

Willy grabbed the seat of his pants, shock registered on his face. "Wait till I tell Ma you . . ." He took one look at his father's face and raised arm, then took off at a run.

"Sorry about that, Miss Bush. I'd be obliged if you'd lend a hand to Dr. McCabe. I'm worried about my wife. She's been ailing these past three weeks."

"Of course," Rose said weakly, reaching for Ben's hand. "I'd be happy to assist in any way I can." She let Ben help her down from the wagon, but the look she gave him plainly said she'd deal with his 'omissions' later.

"Thank you," he mumbled, grabbing his bag and following them into the house. The first hurdle was cleared, but the battle was far from won.

Chapter 36

The room was dark and carried a heavy smell of sickness and vomit. It was stifling, close, and airless. The patient's face was partially hidden under a damp towel across her forehead. Her skin had a greenish cast. Her thin fingers plucked nervously at the blanket pulled up to her chin. She was breathing through her mouth, and every few minutes would swallow hard as though pushing down the urge to use the bucket by the side of her bed.

"Mrs. Backley, it's Dr. McCabe." Ben walked to her bedside and picked up one limp hand, his fingers, in a practiced manner, automatically searching for her pulse. "Mr. Backley," he said over his shoulder, "get some air into this room. And for heaven's sake, empty that bucket."

"Nooo. I need it." As if to give credibility to her words, the frenzied woman leaned over the side of the bed, making dry, retching sounds that produced no results. The effort wracked her body.

She fell back on the pillow, her hand raised. "Horace," she cried out.

"Yes, dear." Mr. Backley took her hand. "Dr. McCabe brought a-a helper with him," he fumbled. "He's here to help, but needs to do an exam before he can make a diagnosis."

"There is no help," she said melodramatically. "I'm dying."

Mr. Backley made a mournful sound, his face wrinkled with fear.

"I see no evidence of your imminent death, Mrs. Backley," Ben said dryly, "although I don't doubt for a moment that you feel terrible. But your husband is right. I have to examine you. However, mindful of your earlier reluctance with me, I have brought my sister-in-law to assist."

"Sister-in-law?" Mrs. Backley's querying voice shot out, nausea forgotten. "You mean, you mean, Miss—" The name appeared lodged in her throat.

"Bush," Ben interrupted brusquely. "Miss Rose Bush has kindly offered to assist. But before we begin, I need to tell you that this will be the last visit I will make to your house if you resist in any way. Or," he added, "if you are rude to Miss Bush. I'm a busy man, and she not only is busy, but she has no reason to extend the hand of kindness to you. What will it be? Do I leave or do I continue?"

"Horace?" she said pitifully, casting sad eyes at the man.

"I'm afraid I agree, dear. We've had the doctor here twice and both times you refused. You're not getting better. In fact, the vomiting continues throughout the day. It does seem to stop in the evening, but starts again each morning. Please. I'll stay right here by your side."

"No, you won't," Ben ground out. "Miss Bush and I are quite capable and don't need to be hampered by your hovering. In fact, instead, I'd like you to brew Mrs. Backley a cup of tea." He didn't take his eyes from Mr. Backley's face. "Now."

Rose bit back a smile at the man's hasty retreat, then crossed over to the window and threw it open, letting in the much-needed air.

She picked up the offensive bucket, and holding it in front of her, arm's length, she marched from the room, returning in a few minutes with a clean, damp towel.

Ben slid up a chair and took out his stethoscope, cupping the end in the palm of his hand. "This might feel a bit cold. It rode in my bag on the way here." He smiled reassuringly at Mrs. Backley and started to undo the buttons on her high-necked gown.

"Stop." Her hand caught his, a frightened look on her face. "I-I can't."

"Of course you can't unbutton them yourself," Rose said soothingly, deliberately misunderstanding her. "I'll just do it for you." Quickly, she opened the gown then took both of Mrs. Backley's hands in hers, holding them securely.

"My," Rose said softly, "you have beautiful hands. Your fingers are long and shapely. Do you play the piano, Mrs. Backley?"

She nodded.

"I thought so. These are the hands of an artist."

"My mother always said my hands were my best feature," Mrs. Backley said proudly, a smug look momentarily replacing the apprehension on her face.

"She was right. Well, only partially right."

"Indeed?"

"Yes. I've often thought your hair was your best feature. It's so thick and such a rich color. Mahogany, don't you think?"

Ben was forgotten and his stethoscope moved across her chest as he listened for heart and lung sounds.

Finished, he folded the instrument and put it back in his bag. He gave a nod to Rose and gently rested his hands on Mrs. Backley's abdomen.

"I would imagine taking care of such an abundance of hair must be quite a chore," Rose mused, drawing back the woman's attention.

"What? Oh, no, not at all. I was brought up with a firm hand, Miss Bush. My mother insisted I do one hundred strokes each night before retiring."

"Mmm, I envy you."

"You do?" she said, surprised.

"Yes, you see I didn't have the good fortune of having a mother in my life. My sister, Petunia, raised us. No wonder you have such refined manners."

Mrs. Backley raised her chin and puffed out her cheeks, basking in Rose's praise. Then, she swallowed hard and glanced toward the empty spot where the bucket had rested.

"Here, let me put this cool towel across your throat. Petunia used to do this for us when we had a stomach upset."

A tear rolled out of Mrs. Backley's eye as she looked at Ben's hands gently palpating her abdomen. "I'm dying, aren't I, Dr. McCabe?"

"No, not at all. In fact, I'd venture to say you're living. Yep, living life to the fullest. Rose, may I speak with you?" He tilted his head toward the door. "Privately."

"Ohhh," Mrs. Backley moaned. "What will happen to my sweet Willy? And-And Horace? They both depend on me for everything." Tears rolled freely down her face, causing her sickly color to glisten.

The door closed softly behind them, then in minutes reopened and Rose stepped back into the room. She went to the bedside and again took Mrs. Backley's hands in hers then leaned over and whispered something into the woman's ear.

Mrs. Backley pulled back her head and gasped.

"It's important, Mrs. Backley. I wouldn't ask if it wasn't necessary. I must know."

"Very well." She cupped Rose's ear as if imparting a great secret.

Rose smiled and again slipped out of the room, returning with Ben and Mr. Backley, who went immediately to the bed and gently put his arm under his wife's head and around her shoulders. Then he rested his head against hers.

"It'll be okay, Mother. Together we can face anything."

"Oh, Horace, I'm so sick. I don't want to die. I don't want to leave you and Willy."

"Have you made a diagnosis, Doc? Do you know what's wrong with my wife?" Tears clogged his throat as his haunted eyes searched Ben's face, wanting to know, yet fearing the answer.

Mrs. Backley's knuckles were white as she gripped her husband's hand.

"I have."

Mrs. Backley gave another pitiful groan.

"Mrs. Backley," Ben addressed the woman, "in about six months you'll . . ."

"Nooo. Six months. I've only six months to live, Horace."

"Mrs. Backley, don't interrupt me again," Ben said, his voice short. But a smile crept around the corners of his mouth.

Mrs. Backley nodded and glanced over at Rose who smiled back reassuringly.

"Miss Bush, how can you possibly smile at a time like this?" Mrs. Backley asked in a wounded voice. "Oh, you must hate me."

"She can because as I was about to say before you interrupted me, in about six months you'll be bringing another Backley into this world."

No one moved. The two occupants on the bed, holding each other, didn't breathe.

"A-Another Backley?" Mrs. Backley repeated in a whisper.

Ben had to lean closer to hear her.

"That's right. You're going to have a baby, Mrs. Backley."

A loud thump sounded as Mr. Backley slid off the bed in a dead faint, his head meeting the floor.

Rose rushed over to him, and Ben chuckled.

"I can't be expecting," Mrs. Backley choked. "The doctor said after Willy there would be no more. I had such a hard time birthing him."

"Well, he was wrong. You've got morning sickness. And unfortunately, yours is lasting all day. I recommend a diet of tea and crackers until that baby of yours settles down and you start eating better and craving all sorts of foods." He walked around the side of the bed and helped raise a pale Mr. Backley to his feet.

"Better take a seat, Horace," Ben said. "Being a daddy is hard work. Let me take a look at your head. Nope, no gash, guess it's harder than the floor."

"A daddy? Did you hear that, dear? I'm going to be a daddy."

"Of course I heard it, you precious man. It stands to reason since I'm going to be a mother."

Ben picked up his bag and motioned to Rose. "I'll be going. I'll check back from time-to-time, but nature will take over from here on out. Don't stay in that bed. Mothers need fresh air and exercise. The nausea will pass."

"I've heard peppermint or chamomile tea is helpful," Rose offered.

Mrs. Backley threw back the covers. "Miss Bush, I'm in your debt. If my baby's a girl, I hope she's as forgiving and kind as you. Horace, I'll need your arm to steady me. You heard the doctor, an expecting mother needs fresh air and exercise."

Chapter 37

Ben and Rose managed to hold back their laughter until the wagon reached the edge of town. Then all it took was one look at each other for it to explode. And after they got the initial bout under control, all they had to do was catch the other's eye and both would dissolve into helpless laughter.

"Oh, Ben, I have to say I envy her. A baby."

"Yep," Ben agreed. "Wouldn't mind one myself. Miss Robin needs some competition."

"Mrs. Backley's a lucky woman."

"Mmm, hmm. But is Wise River?"

Rose gave him a startled look. "What do you mean?"

"Another Willy."

"Ohhh," Rose groaned. "I didn't think of that."

"Bears thinking about all right. But I just think Mr. Backley might find out he's got a backbone after all. Did you see that whack he gave Willy?"

Rose chuckled. "I don't know who was surprised the most, Willy or Mr. Backley."

They both nodded in agreement as they continued back to the Rocking R.

"Ben?" Rose broke the companionable silence.

"Yes." He turned to her.

"I've been thinking."

"Thought you might be. You've been uncharacteristically silent," he teased.

No smile greeted his words. Rose's eyes were fixed down the road as if it contained her answer.

"Rose? I'm listening. And I don't have to tell you, do I, that anything you tell me will be confidential, friend to doctor."

"Thank you, I know that." Rose took a cleansing breath. "Ben, who would you say is the most repulsive, disgusting man in Wise River or even close to Wise River?"

Ben chuckled. "Now that's a question. Why would you want to know?" He then realized Rose was very serious. "Well"—he rubbed his chin—"I'd have to say Elmer Wattle."

"Ugh! I'd have to say you're right. I don't think the man has bathed in years. He looks like he wallows alongside those pigs of his. You can smell his ranch miles before you get there. There's always a plug of tobacco stuck in his jaw, and he spits that vile, brown juice wherever and whenever he wants. I was in the mercantile once when he came in, and I had to hide behind a counter with a handkerchief over my nose."

"He's ripe," Ben agreed, his nostrils flaring.

"I can almost smell him now," Rose said, her face wrinkling into a grimace.

Ben nodded emphatically. "Now, why the question?"

Rose sucked in her cheeks, then said drolly, "Didn't you say it would take a strong woman to make Jesse Rivers overcome whatever keeps him from loving someone? Like me, maybe?"

"I did."

"Well." Rose drew out the word. "How about a strong smell?"

Ben shook his head, a baffled expression on his face. Then his mouth widened into a grin and his eyes filled with glee.

"Damn. Sorry, Rose. But I think I know where you're going with this and I have to tell you—"

"Yes?" Rose asked sweetly.

"It's evil, diabolical, and brilliant. If Elmer Wattle doesn't make Jesse realize the error of his thinking, nothing will. I'd even venture to say that's a stinking thing to do to someone."

Laughter filled the air.

"I couldn't have said it better, Ben. Would you be willing to help me, just a little?"

"I sure would. You're one of my favorite people, Rose, and Jesse deserves a woman like you. What can I do?"

"On your way back to town, would you mind swinging by Mr. Wattle's pig farm? I'd like you to ask him if he'd pick me up tomorrow around eleven o'clock."

"Okay, and why would he do that?"

"Because I want to buy a couple pigs from him, and I need his guidance in picking out just the right pair. Of course, I'll have to visit his farm to do that."

"Whew. Are you sure you can do that? You'll have to throw whatever you're wearing away after being beside him in a wagon. Not to mention the smell of his place. Wear old boots, Rose. You don't know what you'll be wading through."

Rose grimaced. "Oh, I think I have a good idea. Also, you might just let it drop I make the best chocolate cake around. Uh-huh, with thick chocolate icing. And just naturally I'd be bringing him a great big slice to pay for his"—she gulped—"wisdom."

Ben's hearty laugh rang out. "You're a wicked woman, Rose Bush."

"No, just a desperate one."

The next morning when Jesse was in the kitchen for a final cup of coffee, Rose snuck upstairs and slipped on her prettiest dress, one she saved for very special occasions. She would be sorry to see the dress ruined, but it was worth the sacrifice.

The sky-blue gown brought out the azure blue of her eyes, making them hidden pools of promise. Her hair hung down her back, ethereal as spun gold. She put on dainty slippers and pinched her already rosy cheeks. But all the effort and glances into the mirror could not dispel the cold knot in her stomach.

What if it doesn't work? What if I make a fool of myself? Maybe Ben's wrong about Jesse hiding his feelings for me? Maybe he's not hiding them, maybe there's nothing there to hide.

Twice she started down the stairs, and twice she returned to the safety of her room, gulping for air. Finally, she squared her shoulders, placed a smile on her face, and waltzed into the kitchen.

Jesse was busy munching a piece of left over bacon. Tory was the first to see her, and his eyes grew so round they took up most of his face.

"Lordy, Miss Rose," he gasped, "you're beautiful."

Jesse swiveled. His mouth fell open as breath whooshed from him. The bacon fell to the floor.

"Damn," he muttered reverently. He beheld an angel in a blue gown. It was unfair, what she was doing to his heart.

"Awfully early in the day for a dress like that. You going to a p-party?" he stuttered.

"Nope."

"That's sure as heck not a dress you wear to do chores."

Rose forced a quick laugh. "It certainly isn't," she said mysteriously.

His eyes followed her as she moved to the counter then lifted the lid from the cake plate and cut a large slice.

"That's a mighty big slice of cake," Jesse choked out.

Rose gave him a sweet smile. "He's a mighty big man," she said coyly. Then, humming to herself, she wrapped the cake in a square of cloth.

"He?" Jesse gasped.

Rose chose to ignore him, and in a show of anxious anticipation, pulled back the kitchen curtain, gazing out with what she hoped was a longing expression.

As if on cue, a rickety wagon lumbered into the yard. A barrel-chested man pulled back on the reins as angry expletives filled the air.

Rose gulped and ran from the kitchen, making it as far as the door when she remembered the cake. "Oops," she said apologetically. "I'm just so nervous, and excited." A girlish giggle followed the words.

Tory made for the window only to be pushed aside by Jesse.

The sight of Rose, *his* Rose, chore boots in hand, running toward the dilapidated wagon, and the dirty, tobacco-spitting man still spewing cuss words at the hapless mules, caused a few of the same words to spill from his mouth.

"What the hell? That's Elmer Wattle. Stinky Pig Wattle," he added, not believing his eyes.

Knocking a kitchen chair aside, he charged from the room. The smell hit him the moment he opened the door. Mouth ajar, he watched Rose clamber up unassisted into the wagon and scoot close to the foul man.

"Miss Rose." Elmer belched and gave her a nod, his sweat-stained hat bobbing. "Came just like the D—"

"—Just like I knew you would, you, uh, you . . ." Rose swallowed hard. ". . . you big man."

"Huh?" Elmer pulled his short neck back. "Why wouldn't I? I ain't one to shy away from a sa—"

"Slice of cake," Rose hurriedly injected. "A slice of chocolate cake." She tried for an enticing smile. Good Lord, this was harder than she thought.

Out of the corner of her eye, she saw Jesse striding toward the wagon, his face as dark as a thundercloud.

"We'd better go, Elmer," she said with a chortle. "I can't wait to see your farm and your darling little pigs."

"You can't?" he asked disbelievingly. "Best we wait up. Looks like Rivers has something he wants to say."

"No, he doesn't," Rose blurted. And with that, she leaned

forward and smacked the nearest mule's back with one of the boots in her hand.

The mule bucked and the wagon jumped forward, slamming Rose back against the seat.

The startled animals pulled against the traces, made a sharp turn, then galloped out of the yard.

Hair flying, Rose gripped the edge of the seat with one hand and threw a jaunty wave at an unbelieving Jesse.

Chapter 38

Jesse paced up and down, up and down, packing the ground in front of the house. Every few minutes, he stopped and peered down the road. Tory sat on the porch steps, chin in his hand, watching his brother.

"She's been gone two hours," Jesse growled. "She has no business . . ."

"You don't own her, Jesse," Tory said meekly.

"What?" Jesse barked.

"Miss Rose. You don't own her."

"Like hell I don't. I pay her wages. She belongs—"

"To no one," Tory interrupted. "Miss Rose is free to see who she likes." His voice dropped. "She's free to marry anyone she wants, too."

"We'll see about that."

Jesse felt as if his defenses had been stripped away. His emotions were raw. His power of reasoning had fled the moment he saw Rose climb into that wagon and drive away. He caught a glimpse of the future when she'd be climbing into a different wagon and driving away from him for good. He hurt. His whole body hurt.

He stopped in his tracks. "There's no future in it," he said to himself. "I have no right to love her." What he'd just said hit him like a hammer to his stomach. He loved her. How, when, or why didn't matter. He rubbed his hand over his face. The realization filled him with awe. All at once, he knew, without a doubt, the days of hiding behind his fears were over. There was a greater fear at stake. His fear of being the person his father was took second place to his fear of losing Rose. To prevent that, he knew what he must do. He had to cast off the mantle of worry and doubt. He had to tell Rose and hope she'd take him, imperfections and all.

"I'd never hurt her," he said. "I could never hurt someone so precious. I really do love her." The words were weak. Then he spoke them again, stronger, as a smile flashed onto his face. "I'd never hurt her," he shouted the revelation.

Tory jumped to his feet and looked worriedly at his brother. "Jesse?" he asked tentatively. "Are you okay?"

"I'm okay, Tory. In fact, I'm better than okay."

Tory blinked. "If you say so. But I have to tell you, you're acting mighty strange."

"Well, maybe I am. I've been a slow-witted fool." He moved closer to his brother. Then, in a voice full of wonder, Jesse said, "I love her."

"Sure you do." Tory grinned. "I've known that for a long time."

Jesse reached out and ruffled his hair. "How'd you get to be so smart?"

"Well, it sure wasn't from you. Maybe losing Miss Rose isn't smart at all."

"Well, I haven't lost her yet."

"Better tell her that 'cause here they come, and she's wearing a big smile."

Rose's stomach had started doing flips when she'd walked toward Elmer's wagon and the smell accosted her. Still, that was nothing to compare with what it did when she climbed down from the wagon in front of his sagging house and stepped in an oozing pile of pig droppings. Pulling back her foot, she'd swallowed hard and breathed through her mouth.

"Meant to warn you," Elmer said cheerfully. "That's Snout's poop. He ain't particular where he leaves it." He punctuated the words with a loud guffaw.

"Snout?" Rose asked weakly.

"Yep. There he is." He pointed to a large black-and-white boar pig rooting under a scrawny tree.

Hearing his owner's voice, the pig glanced up, and emitting squeals of pleasure, then came running toward them.

"There's my boy. Come here and meet this pretty lady. She's fixin' to buy a couple of your offspring." Elmer chuckled.

"No," Rose protested. "That's not necessary. He doesn't need to . . ." But it was too late. The huge boar was rubbing his long, pink snout against her dress, leaving streaks of what Rose prayed was mud.

"See there, he likes you. Snout's mighty particular who he takes to," Elmer said laconically.

"Lucky me," Rose gasped.

Elmer turned back to the wagon and grabbed the carefully wrapped piece of chocolate cake from the seat.

"Better take this with me. Snout smells it, and he'll find some way to get in that wagon. He purely loves cake. Why, one time I left half a cake on the kitchen table, and when I came back in the room, there he was, big as if you please, standing on the tabletop, snorting it down." He gave a laugh that shook the gut hanging over his filthy pants.

Thus said, he tore open the cloth and shoved most of the cake in his mouth. "Here, Snout, I'll share." He put out his grubby cake-filled paw to the grunting pig. Snout didn't hesitate and happily gobbled down the cake, drools of delight falling between the man's fingers.

"Hey now. Leave some for me." Whereupon Elmer pulled his hand away from the slobbering pig and shoved the remaining few crumbs, drool and all, into his mouth.

"Dang pig's a pig." He laughed uproariously. "Made a joke, didn't I?" He gave Rose such a nudge with his elbow, she stumbled forward into another pile of Snout's indiscriminate leavings.

Rose, stomach rolling, took a deep breath, swallowed, and sent up a fervent prayer she wouldn't embarrass herself by losing her breakfast.

"Well, come on, Miss Bush. We'll go into the pig pen so's you can see the litter I'm, uh, weaning for sale."

Not waiting for Rose, he opened the gate into a pen swimming with mire, soured food slop, and manure from the big sow and her ten prodigies. High-pitched squealing and panic ensued as they ran from the intruders.

"Oh, my." Rose covered her mouth and nose with her hand.

Elmer stopped and looked at her. "Bit ripe, ain't it? You'll get used to it. I don't even smell it anymore. Now you see those two huddled in the corner?"

Rose forced herself to look where he was pointing.

"Them's the last two of this litter ain't spoken for. You want 'em?"

"Huh?" Rose gasped.

"You said you wanted to buy two pigs, didn't you? You ain't been wasting my time now, have you?" He peered suspiciously at Rose. "You're looking mighty peculiar.

"If'n you're spoofin' me, I wouldn't blame you. Most women enjoy my company. No doubt about it, I'm husband material. I'm a wealthy man. I got this fine farm, and I'm in my prime." He leaned closer to Rose, his rancid breath hot on her face. "You probably find me attractive," he said pompously, swelling out his chest.

Rose took a quick step backward, no longer caring what she stepped in. "Oh, no, Mr. Wattle. I don't."

"You don't?" Wonder filled his voice. Wonder and disbelief. "You're a widow woman ain't cha?"

Rose gulped and took another step back. "What I meant to say is, I'm not looking for a husband." At his scowl, she quickly added, "Of course, if I was, I'd consider you." Rose hoped lightning wouldn't strike her for the lie that had just flown from her mouth.

"Figured." Elmer smirked. "Well, you want these two weaners or not?" He might have lost a future wife, but a sale was a sale.

"Uh, sure. Yes, I'm buying them for, for a gift."

"That so?" he asked suspiciously.

"Yes." Rose fumbled. Where was her brain at a time like this? "A gift. A birthday gift," she said. "For Jesse Rivers. His birthday's tomorrow." Breathless, she reached behind her, opened the gate, and backed out.

"Well now, them's a mighty fine gift. I'll deliver 'em tomorrow. You got the money?"

"Yes. Money. I've got it. At home." She made a hasty retreat to the wagon. Readying herself to climb in, she gathered the hem of her gown in her hands only to realize it was saturated with black, smelly mire from the pen.

"Oh, no," she cried, dropping the gown and holding her repulsive hands in front of her face. Without thinking, she vigorously rubbed them down the front of the dress, smearing more of the stinking filth across her bosom.

"Well, get in. Ain't got all day." The wagon groaned and sunk a few inches as Mr. Wattle loaded his girth onto the seat. He barely waited for Rose to climb in before cracking the reins. Missing him by inches, he hollered to Snout to get out of the way as they tore down the rutted road.

Chapter 39

Rose all but fell out of the wagon when it came to a jerking stop a few feet from Jesse. She ducked her head, praying he wouldn't see the tears in her eyes. Hopefully, she was downwind from him.

But her luck had run out. Her feet had no sooner touched the ground than Jesse grabbed her arm and started to pull her to him. Wrinkling up his face, he held her at arm's length and ran his eyes from the hem of her dress to the smears across her bosom. There was even a streak of black mud across one cheek.

"Whew." His breath came out in a whoosh. "Rose Bush, you are one stinking sight."

"Couldn't keep her outta the pig pen," Elmer said. "She was right taken with them pigs. Gotta head back, pert near feedin' time. I'll be bringing the p—"

"Picnic." Rose threw out the word, cutting him off. "You were about to say picnic." Could it get any worse? Now all that she needed was for Elmer to blurt out the real reason for this charade.

"Huh?" He squinted at her then shook his head. Rose Bush was one confounding woman. Good thing she wasn't husband hunting after all.

He snapped the reins, nodded to Rose, still in Jesse's outstretched arms, and said, as the wagon lumbered out of the yard, "Happy Birthday, Rivers. See you tomorrow, Miss Rose."

"Like hell you will," Jesse muttered, then focused his eyes on the woman standing so forlornly in front of him.

"What's he mean, Happy Birthday? And what's this about a picnic?" he growled.

"How would I know?" Rose snapped, trying to break his hold.

"There will be no picnic tomorrow. Elmer Wattle isn't worth your dainty"—he peered down at her boots, covered with excrement—"I was going to say foot, but changed my mind. He's worth every bit what you have on your boots, your dress, your face, and probably even in your hair. You need a bath, lady."

"Why, thank you, Mr. Rivers. I would never have guessed."

"Tory, bring out a couple towels, soap, shampoo, and a blanket. Our pig farmer here is too smelly to enter the house." He dropped her arms. "I'll go around the shed and bring over the tub. You can bathe out here. Good thing the sun's out."

Rose started to protest only to be cut off by a curt order from Jesse, a smile playing around his lips.

"Don't you run off, Rose. I've got some things I want to say to you." He paused, smiling into her eyes. "You really are a stinking mess, my love." Then, holding his breath, he leaned forward to search for a clean spot on her forehead. He placed a tender kiss there. "I'll hurry," he said, hating to leave her. She was even more special now that he'd admitted his love.

Rose couldn't have moved if she'd wanted to. *My love.* The words sang in her heart. He'd called her '*my love*' and, moreover, he'd kissed her. The plan had worked. *Thank you, Elmer Wattle, for making Jesse jealous. She* started to hug herself, saw her hands, and thought better of it.

Tory ran to the house and Jesse, the only thought in his mind the woman waiting, tore around the side of the shed.

He was barely out of sight when Rose heard a loud shout. On the wings of the shout drifted an eye-watering odor.

"What the . . .? Aaugh . . . Get out of here, go on, get," Jesse shouted. "Damn and double damn!" Angry words and ear-splitting expletives smoked the air.

"Jesse," Rose called. "What is it?" Her feet couldn't move fast enough as fear gripped her.

Jesse was in trouble.

"Rose, don't come around the corner of the shed. Stay away," Jesse barked.

"You need help."

"No, I don't. What's done is done. Can't you smell it? Now stay there. The last thing we need is skunk spray mixed with pig manure."

"Skunk spray?" Rose poked her head around the corner of the shed.

There stood Jesse, an arm over his face, fingers pinching his nose. Across from him, tail still raised, stood a very angry skunk. Front legs planted, his black eyes were daring the reeking man to even twitch. Any excuse would do and he'd flip around, lift his tail, and shower Jesse with more of the noxious spray.

"Don't move," Jesse said from between clenched teeth.

"Did-Did he spray you?" Rose asked.

"Can't you smell it? Hell yes, he sprayed me. Thankfully, my pants legs caught most of it."

The skunk stood its ground, raking them with his eyes. The minutes passed in a silence so great they could hear the insects buzzing. Finally, the animal dismissed the two humans as unworthy of further attention and he sauntered into the tall grass and out of sight.

Jesse relaxed, and Rose came running to him.

"You scared me, Jesse Rivers. I thought you'd been attacked."

"Well," he said with a grin, "I was."

"You make my eyes water," Rose said, trying to hide her smile.

"Don't want to hurt your feelings, Rose, but you sure don't smell like your namesake, either." Jesse pulled her into his arms and, laying a finger under her chin, raised her face to his.

"Rose, I have something to say."

"Uh, could it wait until we—"

"No, it can't," he interrupted forcefully. "I have to say it while I have the courage." He cleared his throat. "I swore I'd never love a woman."

"I thought as much," she said forlornly.

"Then you came charging into my life."

Rose opened her mouth.

Hush." He placed a finger across her lips, silencing her. "I've got to get this out, and I don't want interruptions."

Rose blinked back her tears. "I want to hear what you have to say, but I already know what it is."

"You do?" he asked, surprised.

"Yes. You are trying to say as kindly as possible you will never care for me." Rose blinked back the tears. "It's okay, Jesse. That's why I need to leave and that's why . . ."

"Why you decided to entice Elmer Wattle," he finished, a hint of anger creeping into his voice. "I knew you were desperate for your own ranch, but I didn't think for one minute you'd settle for a . . ."

"Pig farmer?"

"Well, yes. We'll discuss that later. Right now, I have more important things on my mind." He took a breath and started again. "I told myself I couldn't love a woman because . . ." He paused, gaining courage to go on. "Because I was worried I'd be like my father. I've been afraid of my temper. Afraid I couldn't control my anger. It would kill me to strike a person I loved."

"But you wouldn't," Rose interrupted. "You are nothing like what I understand your father was."

"No, I'm not, but I didn't realize that until today. Until"—he took her face between his large hands—"until I realized I could lose you. I love you, Rose. I love you with every fiber of my being. With every breath I take. I can't live without you. I need you in my life, here beside me, milking your cow, gathering your eggs, baking in your kitchen."

He took his thumb and wiped the trail of tears now freely running through the dirt on her face.

"I can't promise you we won't fight. We will. We're both independent, strong-willed people. But I can promise I'll never hurt you. And I can promise I'll cherish you until the day I die." He held his breath, his gaze searching her face.

"Jesse, my sweet Jesse. I've loved you forever. I didn't want to. I've been afraid to hope. You can be pig-headed and stubborn. Oh my." She winced. "Did I say pig?"

"You did, right after you said you loved me," he said in a rough voice.

"Well, I do. I couldn't bear the thought of leaving you. It was breaking my heart." She ran a grimy hand down his jaw, her eyes tender, filled with radiant love.

"Then will you marry me? I can't give you a whole ranch, but I can give you half of my share."

"Heck," a voice called from behind them. "She can have half of my share, too," Tory said, grinning.

"All I want is you." She laid her head against Jesse's shoulder, snuggling into his arms, knowing she'd come home. His gentle strength cradling her.

"No pig farm or farmer?" Jesse asked.

"No pig farm or farmer. However, you will be getting two pigs tomorrow. For your birthday." She giggled.

Jesse gave her a perplexed look.

"Well, I had to have some reason for luring the poor man into spending time with me."

"Why on earth would you want to do that?"

"Because, I thought if you saw me with Elmer Wattle you might be jealous." Rose gave him an imploring look.

"You mean you went with that-that man, gave him some of *my* chocolate cake, then came home smelling like a pig wallow, just to make me jealous?"

She nodded. "It was my last hope. Worked, didn't it?"

"Rose, I ought to turn you over my knee."

"You can't. Your knee smells worse than my dress. Neither one of us can go in the house until Tory pours buckets of water over us."

"Then there's only one thing I can do."

"Yes?"

Jesse's mouth found hers and he rained sweet kisses over it and her waiting face. In-between each kiss, he whispered tenderly, "Love you, love you, and love you."

"Hey, you two," Tory called. "The water's waiting. And"—he sniffed—"plenty of soap. It'll take some doing, but if you get to smelling better, I'll allow you in the house. You can sit on the sofa, hold hands, cuddle, and say all those mushy words to each other you want to. Heck, I'll even bring you cookies."

And that's just what they did, far into the night.

Don't miss **DeAnn's** other best-selling books:

UNCONQUERABLE CALLIE

Callie Collins, a proud woman in the late 1800's, is a liar and a darned good one, a master of the dubious art. She is also a dreamer. Her greatest hope is to reach a new life in South Pass City, Wyoming, where she can open a bakery and live an independent life. To be successful, she will need her greatest deception to date, a mythical fiancé who waits at the end of the line. As a woman alone, she has to prove to Seth McCallister, the wagon master, that she has the wherewithal and the stamina to survive months of drought, dust, hardships, and even the risk of death.

Seth McCallister is mystified by the audacity and determination of Callie Collins. His initial distrust and concern for Callie, a woman traveling alone, opens first to admiration, then friendship, then love, a love that he is forced to hold at bay. What he doesn't realize is that there is no fiancé. To make matters worse, Callie develops feelings for Seth McCallister, too. Yet she feels certain that once he realizes her deception, he'll turn away, ashamed of his love and trust in her.

Available now at Amazon:
http://tinyurl.com/nyjgq7m

WYOMING HEATHER

Heather is a spirited, independent woman living alone on a ranch left to her by her parents. She is also a healer of animals, domestic and wild. A woman doing a man's work running a ranch that everyone said couldn't be done, not in this untamed, vastly unsettled land, in the mid 1800's. The ranch had everything she needed except water. She stole that from a neighboring abandoned ranch watched over by a lonely cabin and a grave.

He rode alone coming back after five years to an empty cabin, a run-down ranch, and a grave on a hill. A former Texas Ranger burnt out on life and afraid to love. Whip had spent five years hunting the man that took his wife's life and left him to die.

Whip and Heather meet in an explosive moment on the banks of the Powder River. Both lonely, both drawn to one another, and both fight the attraction.

Available now at Amazon:
http://tinyurl.com/kwrkg5q

TEARS IN THE WIND

Leanna turns her back on the fresh grave of her husband, their small ranch they were forced from by powerful speculators, and hopefully the memories and guilt that torture her. She begins life anew in Wyoming. There, still carrying the secret of her husband's death, she meets wealthy, good-looking rancher, Matt Forrister. Their feelings grow, seasoned by a volatile mix of restraint and passion. Can Leanna free herself from the fears that keep her from embracing a life that is wondrous and rich? Will she learn to love again?

Available now at Amazon:
http://tinyurl.com/n7r2np7

ONE SHINGLE TO HANG

A woman with too much knowledge was at risk for insanity. Her fragile mind couldn't handle it. That's what Lil had been told when she went against convention and became an attorney. The 1800's had fewer women lawyers than women doctors. Her pride knew no bounds when she hung her shingle—L.M. Wentfield, Attorney At Law.

Drew was a struggling cattle rancher, building a fledgling Hereford empire. He was working toward that goal when he was accused of rustling and faced possible hanging. He needed a lawyer—a good one—a man. Chesterfield had one lawyer—a new one—L.M. Wentfield. He wasn't prepared for a beautiful blonde with a sharp tongue and fiercely won independence.

Lil had no homemaking abilities. Her love was the law. And if the thoughts of the gray-eyed cowboy, who had the audacity to refuse her legal help, stayed in her mind, she'd push them aside. She had nothing to offer a rancher . Even her wealth wouldn't be considered an asset to a prideful man. And Drew Jackson was proud. So proud, he knew he couldn't ask a woman of Lil's stature to share his life—but he wanted to—from the moment he'd stolen that first kiss.

Available now at Amazon:
http://tinyurl.com/q9pmsv9

MONTANA MAN

Ben McCabe has only one thing on his mind when he's released from the Yuma Territorial Prison for a crime he didn't commit: Revenge. Four years of his life gone, spent in a torturous hellhole. He wants the man responsible brought to justice, regardless of the cost.

When Wisteria Bush finds an unconscious man next to the Colorado River, she knows she has to help him, no matter how dangerous he may be. She nurses him back to health to find he is a threat to her, but not in a way she'd ever imagined. When her brother takes up cattle rustling and intends to marry her to his boss, the handsome stranger has other ideas.

Available now on Amazon:
http://tinyurl.com/h3zhrgj

Writing as **D.M. Woods**:

DEATH CROSSES THE FINISH LINE

Carrie Preston has a puzzling gift for sensing the motivation and direction of a killer, and homicide Detective Tom Watts is not beyond exploiting her ability. In a pre-dawn phone call, he begins his familiar plea, asking Carrie to join an investigative team stumped by a string of recent murders in the Denver area. Someone is stabbing women to death. Always in health clubs. What is the link between the murdered women? Outwardly fighting against Tom's request, Carrie can't help but feel the inevitable draw—to find the killer, yes, but also to work with Tom Watts again.

Carrie and Tom chase clues throughout Colorado, from Denver to Aspen. But with each successive murder, the killer is a leap ahead of them, leaving a trail of dead bodies. Together they must solve this crime. But Carrie's success is as double-edged as her desire for Tom: What will stop the killer from altering the pattern, from turning toward Carrie as his next victim?

Available now at Amazon:
http://tinyurl.com/lyrus52

DEATH IS A HABIT

Carrie and Tom join together again to track a serial killer bent on eliminating selected petite blondes. Death comes in a takeout cup of deliciously brewed latte. The clues are meager—a cup of latte, a missing lock of hair, and an unidentifiable poison. What is the link between the murdered women? Carrie and Tom fight against a timetable known only to the killer.

Homicide detective Tom Watts isn't beyond exploiting Carrie's particular talent as he lures her back into helping him, needing her gift of perceiving what isn't there, feeling what others refuse to see or acknowledge, and his desire to have her back in his life. He senses Carrie is ready to do combat again after her last brush with a serial killer dubbed The Jock, a harrowing brush with death that left her healing in a hospital bed. Carrie stops fighting Tom's request and joins this man who holds a piece of her heart. What will stop the Latte Lover from deciding that although neither Tom nor Carrie meets his criteria, they could be the next victims?

Available now at Amazon:
http://tinyurl.com/k79z3cd

DeAnn Smallwood:

DeAnn Smallwood lives in Colorado with her husband and their two Yorkies, Stormy and Eli. She is a native of Colorado but has lived in Montana and Wyoming. Her greatest pleasure next to writing is having her books read and enjoyed. Be sure to check out books written under her pen name: D.M. Woods. There you'll find her first two novels in the "Death" series of romantic/thrillers: Death Crosses The Finish Line & Death Is A Habit. She currently has seven western historical romances published, and many more just waiting to be written and shared.

CPSIA information can be obtained
at www.ICGtesting.com
Printed in the USA
LVOW13s1752090818
586506LV00028B/496/P